Praise for *No Dawn for Men*:

"A rousing success, a thrilling adventure that does its clever frame story justice."
– Booklist

"Action-packed from the onset and never slowing down, fans of the two great authors and readers who appreciate a unique superbly-written 1930s thriller will enjoy this unique, tense war drama."
– Midwest Book Review

"Simply UN-PUT-DOWN-ABLE…. Sinister, mystical, comical and daring, *No Dawn For Men* will have you on the edge of your seat from start to finish. A gripping and captivating read that I highly recommended to all book lovers!"
– Reading for Pleasure

"I blasted through this book."
– Cheryl's Book Nook

"If you are a fan of Tolkien or Fleming, then I highly suggest you pick up a copy of *No Dawn for Men*."
– Books: The Cheapest Vacation You Can Buy

"*No Dawn for Men* again proves James LePore to be a superb crafter of thriller novels…. Highly, highly recommended!"
– Crystal Book Reviews

No Dawn
for
Men

James LePore

and Carlos Davis

THE
ST●RY
PLANT

The Story Plant
Studio Digital CT, LLC
PO Box 4331
Stamford, CT 06907

Mass Market paperback ISBN-13: 978-1-61188-297-1
E-book ISBN-13: 978-1-61188-074-8

Visit our website at www.thestoryplant.com
Visit the author's website at www.jamesleporefiction.com

First Story Plant Paperback Printing: December 2013
First Story Plant Mass Market Paperback Printing: March 2021
Printed in the United States of America

0 9 8 7 6 5 4 3 2 1

Acknowledgments

I wish to thank my friend Tom Connelly, polymath and sage, for reading and consulting on various subjects.
— J.L.

I especially would like to thank David Taylor who was there at the creation and ever since. My agent, Gayla Nethercott who is always there. Lucy Buckley for her encouragement and Jennifer Nevins for introducing me to Karen and Jim.
— C.D.

Dedication

We dedicate this book also to the memory of John Ronald Reuel Tolkien and Ian Lancaster Fleming, for the boundless joy they have brought and will forever bring to the world.

To Karen, the First Angel.
— J.L.

For Jamie, my son and sunshine.
— C.D.

PROLOGUE
Ovillers, France
July 15, 1916, 3:00 a.m.

One minute the lieutenant was on all fours, breathing more smoke and tear gas into his lungs than oxygen, his face, legs, arms, and chest covered with the ubiquitous red clay mud of the Somme Valley, and the next he was in a shell crater lying face up along the hot, lathered flank of a horse. On the Roman road the day before, he had seen a multitude of horses and mules in motion, but coming to his senses, realizing he was alive and not in pain, he thought, *impossible.*

"He bolted."

The young officer, startled, turned on his side and lifted his head. Behind the horse, in a ray of moonlight, as if stage-lit, leaning against the rear wall of the crater, was a British major, his mud-covered field tunic ripped open, exposing a milky bare chest. One hand was inside what was left of his blouse. His head was bare. His darkly handsome face was streaked with dried blood.

"It's a head wound," the major said. "Superficial."

"Sir." Indeed the lieutenant could see a two-inch open gash on the major's forehead, just below a fall of wildly disheveled black hair. The gash, a pair of piercing dark eyes, and a full, straight mustache all ran severely parallel. In the soft moonlight, despite the blood and the mud and the ripped shirt, or perhaps as

9

a result of them, he looked more like a London stage actor than a yeomanry major. *Dashing* came to the lieutenant's mind; and then automatically, as Norse languages held a mystical place in his fertile imagination, he thought: *from the Danish* daske—*symbolic of forceful movement. Of course.*

"What are you doing here, Lieutenant?"

German trench mortar shells—sausage bombs his men called them—had been, until a moment ago, whizzing overhead and exploding all over the terraced hillside. One had pulverized, literally, one of his runners only seconds after his platoon had fixed their bayonets and plunged into the darkness. The blast from another must have flung him into the crater. How much time had passed? No matter. The major. What are you doing here? Shell shock, likely. But just how badly was he wounded?

"My kit, sir," the lieutenant said, reaching inside his muddy tunic for the first aid packet sewn into it. *Good luck, it's still there,* he thought as he fingered the contours of the kit, which he knew contained a sterile dressing.

"Don't bother," the major said. "The bleeding's stopped. It's just a gash."

"Sir . . ."

"You can do something for me, though."

"Sir."

"The horse."

"Sir."

"It's got me pinned down, I'm afraid."

The lieutenant got to his knees and crawled around the motionless but still breathing horse to where the major was leaning against the muddy crater wall. Thick clouds, the kind that raced like locomotives across the summer skies above the Somme and dumped endless torrents of rain on the poor souls waging war below, now blocked the moonlight from penetrating into the crater. The major's left leg, to just below the knee, was under the horse's torso. Rain began to fall. The lieutenant, who had lost his

Enfield, his signaling gear, and his tin hat, put his boot against the horse's quivering shoulder, and, with his back to the wet and crumbling wall, pushed, and pushed again, and then again. To no avail. The one-hundred-and-sixty-pound lieutenant was no match for the fifteen-hundred-pound horse. The rain now came down in earnest and he was quickly soaked, as was the major; black and brown dirt from the hillside mixing with the red clay to form a treacly mud that ran down their tunics to reach all the parts of their bodies. The German shelling began again. The hillside was crisscrossed with barbwire. Hung up on it like rag dolls, or crawling about looking for lost limbs, men were crying out all around them.

"Just as I thought," said the major.

"Sir."

"Lieutenant?"

"Sir."

"Do you have any word but 'sir' in your vocabulary, Lieutenant?"

"I have a first in English language and literature, sir. Oxford."

The major barked out a short laugh. "I trust one day you'll put it to use," he said.

"Sir."

"You're a signal officer."

"Yes, sir." The lieutenant fingered his insignia.

"I was a mile away when the shelling started. Can you believe it? The barbwire did him in, or he'd still be galloping, with me hanging on."

They both looked at the horse in extremis, his mouth foaming, his breathing shallow, his eyes bright with fear. Barbwire had cut him in a hundred places. A steady nicking sound could be heard coming from deep within the huge animal's throat.

"I was trying to get a sense of this bloody advance. The moonlight tempted me. I dare say I should not have ventured out."

"How long have you been sitting here, sir?"

"He speaks."

11

"Sir."

"A few hours."

"I'll get help."

"You would be disobeying orders, would you not? No stopping for the dead or wounded."

"Yes, sir."

"What is your objective?"

"A German trench at the top of the hill."

"You can do something for me."

"Sir."

"I've been scribbling." The major took his right hand out of his blouse. In it was an oilskin pouch, which he handed to the lieutenant. "Give it to my wife if I'm found dead here."

"Sir."

"Eve Fleming. The address is there."

"I will, sir. And you are?"

"Valentine Fleming. Queen's Oxfordshire Hussars. Look at the casualty lists."

"Yes, sir."

"One last favor."

"Yes, sir."

"I seem to have lost my revolver. My horse needs to be put out of his misery—he has two broken legs. And I may need it if the bloody Huns send out scouting parties. Take one or two with me to hell. Free of charge."

"I'll do it, sir."

"No, it's my horse."

The signal officer's revolver was still on his web belt. He unsnapped the leather holster, pulled out the gun and handed it to Fleming.

"Thank you. Sorry about the ribbing."

"Sir."

"This rain may be a blessing for once."

"Sir?"

"Loosen the ground. Ease my leg out."

The lieutenant glanced down at the horse, estimating its dead weight. There would be no easing out of the captain's leg. On an impulse he reached behind his neck and pulled a medal he wore on a chain over his head. "Will you take this sir?" he said, handing it to the captain.

"What is it?"

"St. Benedict."

"Papist?"

"I prefer Roman Catholic."

The captain took the medal and studied it, turning it over and over again. "What's this on the back?" he asked.

"*Vedo Retro Satana.*"

"Get thee back Satan?"

"The Hun, sir."

The two men, not far from each other in age, but miles apart in status—military and civilian—looked at each other, acknowledging with their eyes that, as close to death as they both were, formulaic religion meant nothing, and everything.

"We're rather free-form Protestants in my family," the captain said.

The lieutenant had no answer for this. There was no place for free form anything in Roman Catholicism.

"It must be special to you," Fleming said.

"No, sir. I found it in a trench."

The captain bowed his head and slipped the medal around his neck. "Get on with it," he said.

"Sir?"

"The war."

The young signal officer crawled out of the crater. At the rim he heard a shot, just one of many he had heard and would hear among the sounds of exploding shells and cries of pain throughout that mad night, but one he would remember for many years to come.

1.

Berlin
September 26, 1938, 2:00 p.m.

Like a rabid dog, the young and handsome *Reuters* reporter thought as he sat balcony-left looking down
at the top of Adolph Hitler's bobbing head and
snout-dominated profile, the iconic mustache a black
smear above a thin, angry mouth. A mouth spewing
spittle and fire. *The perfect villain.* The reporter and
his colleagues from around the world had been giv-
en a translation of the Fuhrer's speech that morning,
which they had immediately telexed to their news-
rooms. The speech, if you could call it that, was being
broadcast live, with simultaneous translations gen-
erously provided by Herr Goebbels' *Reich Ministry
for Popular Enlightenment and Propaganda* to dozens
of countries around the world. Everyone knew what
Herr Hitler was going to say and what he was indeed
saying. The reporter had come to the Sportpalast for
the spectacle, not the words, and to take pictures.

The front rows of the jam-packed arena were
filled with the *crème de la crème* of the Nazi Party and
the German military. Start there and work your way
back, his SIS contact had told him. So, throughout
Hitler's "we will take the Sudetenland if you don't
give it to us" speech, the reporter snapped away with
the tiny camera hidden in his opera glasses. *Great fun,*
he thought, planning on what he might say if by some

unlucky chance his camera, or its compact film canister, were discovered. *There are more Germanophiles in England than you realize, old chap.* Was Germanophile a word? No matter. He spoke better German than most Germans spoke English. The rough "low" Silesian dialect he affected in general conversation with Germans was something he had picked up during a two-week liaison with an arrogant but sexually inventive "reporter" for the Home Press Division of the Propaganda Ministry while they were both covering a Wagner festival in Leipzig in 1935. Adolph did not attend, but many of his high-level henchmen did, making for a huge harvest of pictures. The reporter, a top-and-bottom natural blond, said she was sleeping with Goebbels and needed a break from his neurotic fretting about his *untreue* to his wonderful Magda. "*Wondervoll Magda* my ass," his friend had said. "She's frigid and bony and he fucks her only out of guilt." "I'm your man," the reporter had said, the same twinkle flickering in his eye as when she smugly identified herself as a reporter. Korrespondent *my ass,* he had said to himself. *Try reporting something critical of Hitler, or the Nazi party.*

"He doesn't want any Czechs *at all,*" the American reporter sitting next to him said. "How fortunate for Mr. Benes."

"Yes, I like the '*at all*' bit," the reporter replied. "I suppose Benes is listening, poor chap. The Czechs are always in the way."

"And Chamberlain and Daladier," the American said. "What will they do, do you think?" But the reporter was not listening. *Fuhrer, command and we will follow!* the crowd, on its feet en masse, was now chanting in one voice, fifteen thousand Germans baying in unison as their mad leader howled at the world. Panning the wildly cheering crowd, the reporter saw ecstasy on its collective face, its thousands of pairs of eyes on fire with lust. *Orgasms,* he thought, *they're having orgasms. These huge Swastika banners, the little dog foaming at the mouth. It's an orgy.*

He stopped his panning abruptly to focus on a tall, handsome brunette in the tenth row center. She was not clapping, but simply standing still and clasping her hands in front of her. Was she grimacing? That would take courage. Had he seen her before? Yes he had. He never forgot a pretty face. She had been at the bar at the Adlon, his hotel, last night, having a drink with a rumpled but distinguished looking older man, Germany's version of the Oxford don. Swiveling left and then right, the reporter snapped pictures of the handsome uber-Aryan men on either side of the brunette. Both were in SS gray, both square-jawed Nordic blonds, both clapping wildly.

"Fleming," his colleague said. "Put those silly glasses down. What do you think Chamberlain will do? He's *your* Prime Minister."

"Are you a dog lover, Dowling?" the reporter replied.

"Excuse me?"

"I daresay most of you chaps are. Americans, I mean."

"Aren't you Brits batty over your fucking hounds? The hunt and all that?"

The reporter smiled. He himself did not like dogs, had indeed avoided them at all costs for as far back as he could remember. "We had a great pack of them," he said. "Have you seen what they do when they corner a fox or a stag?"

"We don't get much of that in Chicago."

"Does it matter what Chamberlain does?" the reporter said. He had, he knew, a reputation for flippancy in the international press corps, of which he was only sporadically a member. To them he was a dilettante, rich and pampered, a reputation he hoped was a result of hard work and not something he naturally exuded. "Look down there," he continued, nodding first at the manic crowd below, and then at their bizarre, Chaplinesque leader, his right arm held high in the Nazi salute, the white-hot flame of the fanatic in his eyes. "In a few days, or a few months, the hordes of hell will be unleashed, no matter what decision Chamberlain takes."

"Madmen and cowards," the American said. "Europe's specialties."

Spot on, the reporter thought, wincing inwardly, surprised, as usual, that his faux arrogance had once again been taken seriously. *Mustn't lay it on too thick, old boy, you may need a friend one day, and who better than this burly Nebraskan with the blond forelock, the ham hands of a boxer, and, I must say, a keen insight into the continental soul?*

2.

**The Old Quad, Pembroke College, Oxford
University
October 3, 1938, 6:00 p.m.**

Professor John Ronald Reuel Tolkien, John to his wife
Edith, John Ronald to his friends, had just lectured
on Beowulf, but his troubled mind had been on the
handwritten manuscript on his desk on Northmoor
Road the whole time. Torn between thinking about it
and thinking about anything but it, he sat on a stone
bench between two very old sycamore trees, a favorite spot of his. Buttoning his worn tweed jacket and
wrapping his woolen scarf around his neck against
the winter-tinged wind blowing across the quad's expansive lawn, he sat under the red and yellow canopy
formed by the autumn leaves overhead, trying to decide. Instinctively, he reached for his pipe and tobacco pouch and was about to set match to bowl when
he noticed the newspaper weighted down by a rock
at the far end of the bench. The wind was ruffling its
pages. The rock did not conceal the headline: **IT IS
PEACE IN OUR TIME**. He had heard the news
of course, had read the *Times*' front-page article on
Saturday. This was the *Daily Mail*, a paper he rarely
read. He picked up the rock, thinking to carry the
paper home to read later, or, more likely, toss it into a
dustbin along the way. Politics did not interest him,

and war—another war—was something he could not bring himself to contemplate.

As he was setting the rock aside, he saw a small square of folded paper stuck to its flat underside. He pulled it off, unfolded it, and saw typed in the very center:

> Þat kann ek it tolfta,
> ef ek sé á tré uppi
> váfa virgilná,:
> svá ek ríst ok í rúnum fák,
> at sá gengr gumi
> ok mælir við mik.

The professor turned the paper over, where it was blank except for the residue of the glue that had been used to adhere it to the rock, then back again.

"Hávamál," someone said.

"Yes, of course," Tolkien answered, his voice a low murmur as he read again the Norse runes.

"And the translation?" the voice said.

"What?" the professor said, turning to his left and seeing a tall trench-coated man standing there in ominous silhouette, his back to the setting sun. "Pardon me?"

"Professor Tolkien. It's me," the man said, "Arlen Cavanaugh."

"Arlie?" Tolkien replied. "Cavanaugh? What are you doing here?"

"I've come to ask a favor, sir. Can you translate that bit?"

"Of course I can."

"Can I stand you a drink, sir?"

3.
Oxford
October 3, 1938, 6:15 p.m.

From his seat in the back of the Eagle and Child pub, —or the Bird and Baby, as it was known around Oxford, —Professor Tolkien watched as his old student, Arlen Cavanaugh, weaved his way, a Guinness stout aloft in each hand, to him. Tall and thin, his blond hair swept back to reveal twinkling blue eyes, pointy ears and a narrow face, his former student seemed to glide effortlessly around and through the knots of people standing, talking and drinking in the crowded pub. Did his feet touch the floor? The professor remembered that Arlie had been a great athlete, swift and graceful on the rugby field, where he seemed never to lose his balance, and the squash courts, where he bested all comers, smiling impishly and barely breaking a sweat the whole match. The word "elven" came to Professor Tolkien's mind, which surprised him since he was used to thinking of elves as smallish creatures.

On the five-minute walk from Pembroke he had had a quick lesson in the improbable. Arlen, a poor student from a rich Midlands merchant family, had, after flunking out of Oxford, wangled an appointment to Sandhurst, where he lasted less than a month, and then managed somehow to land a job in Naval Intelligence, where he now worked directly under its director, a man named Hugh Sinclair, who Arlie referred to as Uncle Quex. SIS, MI-6. *Quite.*

"Why the note under the rock?" the professor asked when Arlie was seated.

"I was just having fun. You know me."

"That's why you were sent down, Arlie."

"No doubt, sir."

"What's your interest in Hávamál?" The professor had pulled the note out of his pocket and spread it on the scarred wooden table.

"We think Herr Hitler is interested in it as a code book."

"That's absurd," John Ronald replied. "It would be easily deciphered."

"Decoded, actually."

The professor, now forty-six and with World War One between him and his youth, rarely recalled his undergraduate days with anything but pain. Two of his best friends lay buried in the Somme Valley. He smiled now though, thinking of the brashness of the TCBSers, as he and his small coterie of public school classmates called themselves, not unlike the brashness of Mr. Cavanaugh.

"So you're lecturing me now," he said, trying unsuccessfully to turn his smile into a frown of mild indignation.

"No, sir. Just correcting your usage. Codes are decoded, ciphers are deciphered."

"Is this what you're learning at Bletchley House?"

"Yes, sir. Among other things."

"Excellent. Learning something."

"We had the same thought," Cavanaugh said, "about Hávamál. The Germans have Enigma machines. They are well beyond code books."

"Should I still be worried about German aggression?"

"Professor . . . Are you serious?"

"I was rather hoping the headlines were accurate."

"There's no chance of that. Hitler's a madman."

"Are you sure?"

"*They have seen my strength for themselves, have watched me rise from the darkness of war, dripping with my enemies' blood.*"

"My God, Arlie. You were listening."

Silence, and a disarming, boyish smile from Arlie; then, the smile short-lived, the young man's face suddenly deadly serious: "He's killing Jews by the thousands. He's arming himself to the teeth. Uncle Quex says he'll invade Poland next year."

"And what is it you need of me?" The quote from Beowulf had penetrated the professor's defenses. He had learned about evil on the Somme and did not want to believe that its great dark shadow was again falling over the world. But of course it *was*. And here was a young man some might consider intellectually challenged to remind him, to jar him from his personal struggle with what was, after all, just a novel, a fiction, epic though he hoped it might be.

"Do you know a Professor Franz Shroeder?" Cavanaugh asked.

"Franz Shroeder? Yes. He taught one term at King Edward's when I was there."

"He's a top man in his field."

"Correct. Norse Mythology, of which Hávamál is a core text."

"He's retired, I believe."

"I hadn't heard that."

"Or on a long sabbatical."

"You can get to the point, Arlie. Indeed, having heard Grendel's words fall from your lips, I am eager to know what it is."

"You're going to Berlin on Wednesday, to talk to a publisher, I believe. A German translation of *The Hobbit*."

"You believe?"

"I know."

"What else do you know?"

"You have a five-day visa."

"Correct."

"Shroeder is working on something on direct orders from Himmler. We'd like you to help us find out what it is."

"Who is Himmler?"

"The head of the SS, Hitler's political police. A nasty bunch. The Gestapo comes under his command. You've heard of them of course."

"I have. Difficult to avoid hearing of them from time to time. How would I do this—discover what Shroeder is working on?"

"*The Hobbit* is popular in Germany, among those who read English. It appears the German-only readers are clamoring for a translation. Shroeder is something of a celebrity there at the moment because of the Nazis' obsession with runic symbols and all that Aryan nonsense. We've arranged for you to meet with Professor Shroeder. 'Famous Dons Discuss the Norse Gods and Middle Earth.'"

"I see. Are you wincing, Arlie?"

"Inwardly, yes."

"You should be." Tolkien retrieved his pipe and tobacco from his jacket pocket and proceeded to fire up. It was a comfort to him, this ritual, and also an excuse to think. *Who is Himmler? Indeed, where have you been, John Ronald?* "It's a children's book," he said, finally.

"Perhaps," his former student answered. "But there are certain . . . the Nazis seem to like it."

The Professor, drawing on his pipe, raised his eyebrows and then lowered them slowly. Bloody Nazis, he thought, surprising himself. He had, he realized, been so miserable over his writer's block and his London publisher's failure to see reason that he had forgotten to pay attention to the real world, which was obviously careening toward disaster. *Cease the self-indulgence, John,* he said quietly to himself. *Cease and desist.* "Go on," he said out loud.

"There will be stories written," Cavanaugh continued, "for UK and German consumption. The

Reuters man will be working with you. The Nazi Propaganda Ministry is all in."

"All in?"

"Yes, it's a gambling term."

"Ah, are you a gambler, Arlie?"

"I'm afraid I am."

"What *Reuters* man?"

"His name is Ian Fleming. He's in Germany now, covering Munich, the annexation."

"How will we accomplish our objective?"

"We have a simple plan."

"As simple as there and back again, I suppose."

This time Arlie Cavanaugh did not get the reference. So much for an author's pride. Or did he? He was hunching forward now, his blue eyes twinkling again, ready to explain.

4.

Berlin
October 4, 1938, 6:00 p.m.

"Fraulein Shroeder, please permit me to introduce myself." The brunette, sitting in a plush chair in a nook of the Adlon's luxuriously appointed lobby, turned and looked directly at Fleming. Her heart-shaped face, up close, was not just pretty, it was dazzling. Wide-set, dark brown eyes, a clear brow, a straight nose with slightly flaring nostrils, full lips painted a subtle but sensuous red. *Not yet twenty-five*, the Englishman said to himself, *perfect.*

"I am not accustomed to being approached by strangers," the young beauty said, smiling and extending her hand, "but in your case, Mr. Fleming, I feel I can make an exception."

Fleming stepped closer, took the extended hand, and kissed it gently, lingering perhaps a half-second longer than was entirely appropriate. *What is that scent?* He asked himself. *Jasmine? Gardenia? Careful, old man, careful. She's a thoroughbred.*

"I did send my card up," Fleming said.

"There was no need. Your kind Ambassador paved the way."

"Old Nev. He and my father were good friends."

"So he said."

"Did he say anything else?"

"He said you used a tortoiseshell cigarette holder and were dark and charming."

"He . . ." Fleming, who was smoking one of his Morland's Specials, arrested his hand in mid-motion to look at his cigarette holder. Then he smiled. *Clever girl,* he said to himself, *could she be flirting?* No, just youthful exuberance. *Feisty filly, tweaking the superior male, the upper class Brit.* Another smile, a slight nod of acknowledgment. "You don't mind spending a few hours with me, then?" he continued.

"A few hours? I was told Professor Tolkien would be here for five days."

"I shall try not to make a nuisance of myself. How is Professor Shroeder disposed to our plans?"

"Extremely well. Delighted, in fact. Of course he doesn't understand why there is thought to be the slightest interest in his work."

Fleming had taken the seat across from Miss Shroeder, eying her long, graceful body under her perfectly fitted cocktail dress, an understated but expensive frock, he could tell, black, with simple but striking white and pale green piping at the throat and cuffs. While they were talking he had raised a finger to a passing waiter, who now returned.

"A drink, Fraulein?" Fleming said.

"Three fingers of St. George's," Ms. Shroeder said. "Neat."

"I'll have the same," Fleming said. "With a chunk of ice."

"Head in the clouds, I daresay," Fleming said, when the waiter had gone. "Your father, not the waiter." Miss Shroeder smiled. "Seriously," Fleming continued, "I'm told Herr Goebbels' people are delighted with the prospect of such good publicity for the fatherland. Your father's work is apparently very important."

"And this," the young woman said, "will have the added benefit of actually being true."

"I daresay."

"You are surprised that I would speak so of Herr Goebbels?" Fleming had raised his eyebrows for a split second. Now he smiled. "I saw you at the Sport-palast last week," he said.

"Ah, the Fuhrer in all his glory. And now we have the Sudetenland and we shall have peace in our time."

"One hopes." Fleming had no hope. He had popped into a *kino* on Unter den Linden after tea to see just how good Herr Goebbels was, and had there seen a beautifully choreographed newsreel of Nazi might crossing the Czech border. *5:45 A.M., October 4, 1938, The Sudetenland Is Regained!* Hitler had gone in fifteen minutes ahead of schedule, unable to control himself. And in ten hours Goebbels had produced a professional looking film and distributed it in time for a five o'clock showing all over Berlin.

"Yes, one hopes," said Fraulein Shroeder. "*I* hope we will have the chance to talk while you are interviewing the two professors."

"I as well."

"Good. *Gut.* You can tutor me on the subject of British politics. I am fascinated by it."

"And on what subject will you tutor me?"

"I have no specialties, unfortunately. I am too busy caring for father."

"You must have one or two secret passions."

"One, yes, but I do not believe I can share it with you, or anyone. We shall see."

"*Comment intriguant, madamoiselle.*"

"No, not really."

"Well, until tomorrow then . . ." Fleming got to his feet and extended his hand. "My dear . . ."

"It's Billie, for Lillian."

"May I?"

"Of course."

"Billie for Lillian," Fleming said, smiling, "a beautiful name."

Before he could kiss her hand and take his leave, however, a distinguished looking, white-haired gentleman and a very short, stocky man with red-dish-brown hair and a long, thick beard of the same color approached them from behind Miss Shroeder.

The small man's beard was entwined into two plaits in the middle. The old man, in rumpled tweeds, was using a cane and had his free hand on the small man's shoulder. "Can this be . . . ?" he said.

Billie, a quizzical look on her face, turned to look behind her, then rose swiftly and reached both of her perfectly manicured hands out to the older man. "Father," she said, drawing him to her and kissing him on the cheek. "You're in time to meet Mr. Fleming. And Trygg, what a happy surprise. Professor Franz Shroeder, Mr. Ian Fleming. And this," she continued, nodding down at the little man, "is Mr. Trygg Korumak, my father's valet and sometimes major domo of our rather small house in Heidelberg."

"It's a great pleasure," Fleming said, shaking hands with both men, noticing that Korumak's hand was large and hairy and his grip like a vice. Under four foot, Fleming thought, but with a chest like an ape and long arms to match. Eyes like a panther's. Intelligent, shrewd eyes for all that. What was he, a dwarf, a midget? A circus freak? "I was flying off. I'll leave you to yourselves."

"Don't you want to discuss tomorrow's business?" said Professor Shroeder. "Perhaps assign me some homework?"

"Shall I arrive an hour early tomorrow? I have done some reading on Odin and that lot, but you can tell me what to ask."

"What about Professor Tolkien's book. I have supposed it would be inquired about."

"Have you read it, professor?"

"Of course."

"Are you favorably disposed?"

"It's not what Herr Doctor Goebbels thinks it is."

"I see, but do you . . . ?"

"It's charming."

"Excellent. That word and others like it will make everyone happy. Good evening then."

* * *

On his way into the bar, Fleming noticed that the young blond man in the gray suit who had been watching them over an open newspaper from the opposite corner of the lobby, had risen from his plush chair—everything was plush in the Adlon; that's why he loved it so—and was making his way circuitously toward the Shroeders. Was he one of the young Huns who were bracketing her at the Sportpalast last week? A suitor? A watcher? Perhaps both. The SS was sly that way.

5.

Lanstrasse 8, Berlin
October 4, 1938, 8:00 p.m.

Three men in black SS uniforms with Norse runes that looked like double lightning bolts on their tunic collars sat in the dark in oversized chairs in a spacious, marble-floored, epically-appointed room on the ground floor of the newly constructed headquarters of the Ahnenerbe: a society, as its founder Heinrich Himmler liked to put it without the slightest trace of irony, for the study of *die götter, die uns vorausginge*—the gods that preceded us. Himmler, the head of the SS, Germany's one-million-man strong political terrorists, was one of the three men. The others were Karl Wolff, Himmler's chief of staff, and Reinhard Heydrich, the head of the Gestapo, the SS's secret police. They had just listened to a presentation, with slides, by Walther Wust, the president of the Ahnenerbe, an intellectual turned Nazi, and were now drinking hock, a white wine from the Rhine Valley that the SS chief favored when he allowed himself a moment of leisure. Himmler himself had risen, dismissed Wust, flipped on two nearby lamps, closed the oak doors of the large custom-built cabinet that held the screen, and poured the wine.

"Heil Hitler," Himmler said, raising his glass. The other men followed suit and they drank.

"I fear that our explorations are lost causes," the SS chief said, his face grim. Wust, sweating the entire time, had spent forty-five minutes detailing to his superiors the various expeditions either financed by the Ahnenerbe or undertaken directly by it, to remote parts of Finland, Sweden, Germany's Murg Valley, even Antarctica, over the past several years. Wust was eager to report that all of this trekking about with backpacks and small shovels had confirmed that the Nordic race had been the precursor to all great civilizations, including ancient Rome and Egypt. As to the true purpose for all these expensive, tedious-unto-death undertakings, Wust could not help but report that nothing of value had been found. Hence the sweating.

"What about the crone in Karelia?" Heydrich asked. "Wasn't she thought to be promising?"

Himmler shook his head. He rarely showed emotion, which to him would be a sign not of weakness but of sloppiness, which he detested. That was why he wore one of his many severely-cut, buttoned-to-the-top SS uniforms at all times, and why he shaved and trimmed his Hitler-mimicking mustache every day, sometimes twice per day. It was obvious now, though, that he was not happy. "We brought her here," he said. "To the basement. She could not perform."

"Where is she now?" Wolff asked.

"Dachau." Himmler actually smiled. "The wrong politics."

"What about the crystals, the texts, those caves in Sardinia?" said Heydrich. "Nothing?"

"Nothing. Which leaves us with Herr Professor Shroeder," said Himmler. "What is the latest?"

"The old man's valet has arrived from Heidelberg. He's a dwarf. He goes by the name Trygg Korumak."

"Norwegian?"

"We don't know."

"Where is he staying?"

"He's sleeping in a utility closet at Hermann Goering Strasse."

"Is that wise?"

"Shroeder has trouble managing. The valet helps him dress, answers the phone, sometimes walks with him, watches over him."

"Why hasn't he been here sooner?"

"He just appeared last night."

"Where has he been? Who is he?"

"We are investigating, but it appears he has been with the old man on and off for many years."

"Was he on the scene when we recruited Shroeder?"

"No, this is the first we've seen or heard of him."

"A dwarf, you say?"

"Yes."

"Another cancerous growth."

"Yes."

"Soon to be eliminated."

"I could not agree more."

"You are keeping an eye on him?"

"Of course."

"And the excavation at Externsteine, what is the status?"

"They are working around the clock."

"How much longer?"

"Perhaps a week. There are several deep caves that must still be breached and explored."

"Perhaps Herr Professor Shroeder is toying with us," said Himmler. "Perhaps he thinks he is being clever." Himmler had kept his face expressionless, his eyes and voice flat as he took Heydrich through this interrogation. Though fully aware that he was short of stature and ghostly pale rather than fair of skin, the bespectacled Himmler saw himself as a modern Aryan god, to be feared, as Hitler was feared, precisely because he stood out from the blond crowd. He had the power, he knew, to induce not just fear, but crippling, paralyzing fear. Even Heydrich, favored by the Fuhrer, who called him the man with the iron heart, cowered in his presence.

"He knows the consequences," Heydrich said, his lips taut.

Himmler's face softened. He liked to keep Heydrich guessing and often played him off against Wolff and others. This tactic he had learned, and honed, by studying the top god in the Nordic pantheon, Adolph Hitler. He had heard that the Fuhrer did not think much of his efforts to aid the upcoming war effort. A body blow, this. Hitler had never spoken of a successor, but to bring him a weapon of such immense power would surely place him next in line. Professor Shroeder must be made to produce results, and very soon.

"You have handled him and the daughter well," he said, finally. "But Externsteine will be their last chance. Shroeder will have to produce proof soon. Does he know this?"

"He has been told that if he cannot show us something positive in the next week or so, we will shut him down and keep our promise concerning the daughter."

"*Gut*," Himmler said. "We are nothing if not good at our word."

"He is to have a visitor tomorrow, I understand," said Wolff. "The Oxford don."

"Yes, and all approved by Goebbels," said Heydrich. "The meddler." The word meddler—*unbefguter*—he spit out.

"He cannot meddle in something he knows nothing about," said Himmler. "To defy him would be to alert him. And that we do not want."

"I suppose we will have to lose a few days while the two professors talk their nonsense," said Wolff.

"Perhaps Herr Professor Tolkien knows where the magic amulet is," said Heydrich.

"Reinhard," said Himmler, "do I detect a hint of sarcasm in your voice? Have you your doubts?"

"No, Reichsfuhrer. But I am suspicious of Shroeder for more basic reasons. He hates us, as you know. He could not hide his feelings when we first presented the project to him. He may have it in mind to actually use this magic against us."

"My dear Reinhard," said Himmler. "I don't imagine he would be hard to control. He is seventy-eight and doddering."

Himmler, trying not to blink, removed and cleaned his thick, rimless glasses while waiting for Heydrich to answer. It was all well and good that Heydrich was a favorite of Hitler's, but it was *he*, Himmler, who had given him his start, elevated him swiftly through the SS ranks, and made him the head of the Gestapo when Goering was shunted aside. *He* who had pushed for the passage of the Gestapo Law in 1936, a law that allowed Heydrich's people to arrest and detain indefinitely anyone they chose, on suspicion of criminal activity that they had unbridled power to define. No judicial review, no quaint concepts like *habeas corpus*. Many were never seen or heard of again. In Germany you could be arrested because the Gestapo did not like the way you looked. Or smelled. Or dressed. On the streets of Berlin one did not make eye contact with strangers, a state of affairs that made political control a simple matter. *My Honor Is Loyalty* was the SS's motto. No, Heydrich would cooperate, no matter how much he loathed the intellectual, Nazi-hating Professor Shroeder.

"How can we be certain . . . ?" Heydrich spoke, finally.

"Of what, *mein fruend*? That these two old men will find a way to upset our plans, that they will suddenly become heroic?"

"And the English reporter?"

"Goebbels is right. It will be as if Mr. Fleming is working for us, such will be the tenor of the story he sends home."

"And if he learns the truth?"

"Then he dies, and we place Herr Shroeder under house arrest until his work is done. You have your agent in place. Nothing will go wrong."

Silence.

"Don't worry, Gruppenfuhrer," Himmler said. "I will take full responsibility." *And also full credit, full glory,* Himmler said to himself, replacing his glasses on his nose and reaching for the hock.

6.

The Bavarian Forest, Near Deggendorf
Germany
February 11, 1872, 4:00 p.m.

"Franz," young Ernst said. "It's cold."

"It won't be long."

"He's not coming."

"You can go if you wish."

"How will he get down there?"

"I told you, he comes in through that wall on the left."

"It's solid rock."

"No, there, at that ledge where those scrubby bushes are growing, there's a cave entrance. I saw him enter from there both times."

"You mean there's a tunnel from the forest floor."

"There must be."

"How did you find this place?"

"I told you, I was looking for cliffs to climb. This looked likely. Before I could start down, I saw Adelbert emerge with the lynx."

"Have you seen the entrance?"

"No. *Shush.*"

I never should have brought him, young Franz Shroeder said to himself. The boys, age twelve, were in the forest about a half-mile south of their gymnasium at Metten Abbey. Lying on their stomachs on the edge of a cliff, they were looking down perhaps fifty feet into what appeared to be a small, four-sided canyon, on the floor of which stood a circle of sapling oaks surrounding a black, anvil-shaped stone. Behind these slender young trees stood an oak tree of giant proportions. A ten-foot-in-diameter monster of a tree, it towered above the canyon, its naked branches so thick and spread so wide they nearly blocked out the sun setting behind it. Many thick branches reached like skeletal hands toward the boys. Franz could slide on his belly right into the heart of the mother oak if he were so inclined.

They were waiting for Father Adelbert, their Latin tutor.

"We have trekked out here for nothing," Ernst said.

"He will come."

"Why do you say that?"

"I told you what happened last week."

"The lynx could not have been dead."

"I saw the blood in the snow."

"It was wounded."

"You can't deny that he has been slowly going mad."

"People go mad. My aunt Hilda is in an asylum in Switzerland. She killed her baby."

They had hiked through the fields behind the abbey and into the great forest, snow-covered and deadly silent this gray mid-winter Saturday, giving the canyon and its towering ancient oak a wide berth so as not to alert the young Benedictine monk with the pock-marked face and the glowing eyes of a martyr, or a lunatic.

"It will be dark soon."

"Go."

"No.

"Hush. There he is."

Pressing themselves as flat as they could against the snow-covered earth, the boys watched Father Adelbert, his cowl hiding his face, emerge through a small arched opening on a ledge to the left, perhaps thirty feet above the canyon's floor, stumble down the bramble-covered hillside, approach the tree circle then enter it. Something—a small animal—was slung around his neck like a stole. At the black stone he bowed his head and—with reverence it seemed, or fear—slowly uncoiled the animal and placed it on the stone. They saw now it was a dog, one of the mongrels that lived in and around the abbey's stables. A spotted thing that they sometimes fed at a rear door when they had kitchen chores. Its head was bashed in, dried blood sticking to fur and bone where an ear had once been.

The monk knelt facing the stone. He turned his hood down, then removed what appeared to Franz to be a rolled parchment from inside his long brown habit. He untied its leather string, spread it open, and, raising his face to the mother oak, he began to read.

7.

Berlin
October 5, 1938, 6:00 p.m.

"Professor Shroeder."

Professor Tolkien watched the elder don's eyes refocus, as if he were emerging from a trance, which indeed seemed to be the case. Was it the music, a Wagner opera, ebbing and flowing quietly from the tin amplifying horn of Shroeder's Victrola, that had carried him away? Or was he just getting more absentminded? John Ronald remembered how, during his lectures at St. Edward's those many years ago, the German, then only in his forties, his accent thick and comical to his sixteen-year-old students, would often stop mid-sentence and look down at the floor, his train of thought uncoupled for an awkward moment or two.

"Ahem."

"Yes, Professor. I am here."

"What did you see?"

The two men were alone in Franz Shroeder's study in his apartment on Hermann Goering Strasse, not far from the Adlon. Shroeder rose from his chair and went to the fireplace, where he pulled aside the protective screen and poked at the large fire blazing there. "I'll add another log," he said, raising his voice, as if Tolkien were far off someplace and not sitting in a chair a few feet away. "It's cold in here."

After completing this task and replacing the screen, the German walked casually to the polished walnut bookcase on the far wall, on which sat his old fashioned talking machine, and slowly turned the horn toward the wall. Then he turned to face his English visitor.

"The dog stood up," he said.

"Stood up? You mean he wasn't dead."

"He tottered a bit on the stone," Shroeder said, "then howled at the tree, the giant oak. Then he bounded off."

"Professor Shroeder . . ."

"I have never forgotten that howl."

Professor Tolkien was familiar with all of the Norse mythology that concerned itself with the raising of the dead. Indeed, the rune that Arlen Cavanaugh had hidden under a rock as a juvenile way of piquing his interest was a spell that, legend had it, was used by the god Odin to resurrect a man who had recently been hanged. One interpretation suggested it may have been himself he was referring to. But of course, except for Jesus' raising of Lazarus, no historical example of this occurring had ever been recorded.

"How old were you?"

"Twelve. Ernst ran off."

"What did *you* do?"

"I hadn't noticed that Father Adelbert had fallen, he lay sprawled in the snow."

Professor Tolkien rose and crossed over the thickly carpeted floor to warm his hands at the fire. It *had* gotten cold in the room despite the roaring blaze. Shroeder joined him. Looking over, turning his not old, but no longer young-looking hands this way and that, Tolkien took a moment to observe the old German's craggy face in profile, the large nose and protruding brow fighting for prominence, the chin square and proud, the one visible eye black and looking toward a distant, unseeable horizon. A thousand-mile stare. His long white hair seemed somehow windswept, or electrified, a ragged halo above his head rather than on it. *Is this me in thirty years?* Tolkien, who had turned forty-six in January, asked himself. *Shall I be distinguished looking but losing my wits when I am seventy-eight or so?*

"What did you do, Franz?" the English professor gently asked. "May I call you Franz?"

"Of course. My friends call me Franz. Not that I have many. I feel you are my friend."

Tolkien remained silent.

Shroeder turned to face Tolkien. "You will think me mad, if you do not already."

Silence, except for the music, which was barely audible now. Tolkien longed for his pipe, which was on the small, ornately carved table next to the leather-cushioned chair he had been sitting on, a matter of a few steps. But it could wait. *The dog stood up.*

"I climbed down into the canyon," the German don said. "I was a climber as a boy, a passionate free climber, mostly in the summers around home. I found a way down. Thinking back, I don't know how I did it. The walls were nearly sheer, but I must have found enough natural crevices. At the bottom, I knelt beside Father Adelbert. He was dead, his face in rictus. White as a ghost. He was clutching something in his right hand. I pried it open." Shroeder stopped speaking and went behind his desk. He removed a key from the key pocket of his vest—both men were dressed in rumpled tweed suits with vests—bent down and used it to unlock what Tolkien was certain was secret a drawer. A drawer inside a drawer perhaps, or behind a false panel.

"Here," Shroeder said, handing him a small, heavy object. It was a figurine, perhaps two centimeters by two centimeters, of a man sitting on a throne, his face the face of a beast, his hands, resting on the throne's arms, talons. The recessed eyes were deep red gems that emitted tiny glints as the light from the fire caught their surface. It was made of black stone and it was heavy, much too heavy for its size. Was it getting heavier in his hand? He realized he could barely keep it aloft and that the muscles in his arm were beginning to painfully constrict. The Englishman placed the figurine on the desk, his movement abrupt. Was that vertigo he felt?

"What is it?" he asked, still feeling slightly dizzy, his arm aching, all thoughts of the old German's failing wits banished, replaced by other thoughts, confusing unnamable thoughts.

"I don't know."

"What is it made of?"

Shroeder did not reply. He shook his head, then picked up the figurine and quickly returned it to its hidden compartment, replacing the key in his vest. "I have the parchment as well," he said, when he had completed these simple tasks.

"What are you saying, Franz?"

"Do you know this opera?" Shroeder asked. "*Gotterdammerung, the Twilight of the Gods?*"

"Not as well as I should, I fear."

"The story of the ring of power. The Nazis love it."

"Franz, that figurine . . ."

"Sit, Professor Tolkien. I am not insane, though I wish I were. Sit. I will tell you."

8.

Berlin
October 6, 1938, 10:00 a.m.

"Are you a member of the party, Billie?"

"Why do you ask?"

"You don't seem the sort."

"I'm not."

"Not the sort, or not a Nazi?"

"Neither."

Fleming paused to reflect. The sun was full out and though there was a nip in the air, they had decided to sit outside, choosing a café near the Brandenburg Gate, not far from the Adlon. He was very happy to hear that Billie Shroeder was not a Nazi. Stunning, with the sunlight on her face, her teeth alone enough to break your heart, he would have hated to have another tedious moral struggle. He had rationalized away his reservations before, concerning fascist woman—a rapidly growing demographic what with Hitler, Stalin, Franco, Mussolini, and God knew what other monster about to rise from the slime—but the taste it had left in his mouth was not a good one. Morland's Specials, pink gins, and a freedom-loving female were the best purgatives.

"And your father?"

"No, neither."

More good news. How, now, to work that fact into the article? For he actually *was* going to write a

Tolkien-Shroeder story as part of the bargain reached in order to get him and Professor Tolkien access to the German don. *English Don and Non-Nazi German Counterpart* . . . Fleming smiled. *You'll have to do better than that, old man.*

"And Mr. Korumak?" the Englishman asked. "I don't take him for a Nazi."

"He's not."

Fleming paused, pondering whether or not to ask the next question.

"He's an enormous help to my father," Billie said.

"I saw evidence of it last night. How long has he been with you?"

"My father met him when he was very young, still at gymnasium in Deggendorf. But he's not *with* us, exactly; he comes and goes."

"Where does he go when he goes?"

"He has family in the Bavarian Alps, near Nebel-horn, I believe."

Fleming did some math in his head, but decided not to ask the next question. Korumak looked to be no more than fifty.

"I can see you are happy we are not Nazis," said Billie, breaking into the Englishman's thoughts.

"Of course. Such pompous asses, don't you think?"

"You're being kind."

"How have you been able to avoid them?"

"We were in our burrow in Heidelberg far away from the center of things."

"You're here now. Surrounded I should say."

They both looked northward up Unter den Linden towards the Adlon. On their stroll to the café they had seen trucks unloading ten-foot high concrete Doric columns—pedestals—which workmen were now lining up at intervals on both sides of the famous avenue. Other workmen were busy setting golden Third Reich Eagles, their talons clutching a wreath of oak leaves encircling a swastika, atop each one.

They turned back to each other and their eyes met. "Surrounded," Billie said. There was such a look of vulnerability in Billie Shroeder's large brown eyes as she said this that Fleming's heartbeat sped up for a split second, a sensation too strange, too *outre*, for him to contemplate at this moment.

"How did you end up here?" Fleming asked.

"Father was asked by a historical society to help with a research project. They offered him an apartment in Berlin and a small stipend."

"What society is that?"

"The Ahnenerbe."

"Sounds important."

"It's Himmler's brainchild, our Aryan roots and all that nonsense."

"Does Professor Shroeder think it's nonsense?"

"Yes."

"Why is he doing it? Don't tell me. I already know."

"You don't say no to Himmler," they said in unison. Their eyes met and they smiled the grim smile of people who know that there is evil afoot, that the world had gone mad.

"He seems old to be your father." Fleming had paused before making this statement, remembering the pictures he had seen at Bletchley House, the bio he had memorized. No mention of a wife. Sticky.

Now Billie paused and looked down at her coffee cup.

"Forgive me . . ." Fleming said.

"There is nothing to forgive," she said, raising her head. He had feared he would see anger in her eyes, or pain—another surprise, this fear—but no, what he saw was sadness, a momentary revelation of a small piece of her childhood. He hoped it was small.

"My father and my mother were betrothed. He left for England to teach. She died giving birth to me while he was away. He was not aware . . . He returned and raised me in Heidelberg."

"You mean she never told him she was . . . ?"

"No."

"Are you named for her?"

"Yes, but her family severed all ties. They were old Prussians, unbending."

"So you . . ."

"I don't even know who they are, and I'm not interested."

"That Prussian blood."

Billie's smile returned in full. She got the point. *Blood tells.* "You may be right."

"Why are you staying in a hotel, may I ask?"

"They are enlarging the apartment, making a room for me and a larger study for father. They've put me up at the Adlon until the work is done."

"So you and Professor Shroeder will be in Berlin for quite a while."

"I long for Heidelberg, but yes."

"Shall we take a ride there when these interviews are over?"

"That would be lovely. It's beautiful country."

"How did your father and Professor Tolkien get on last night?"

"I don't know. I rang him this morning, but there was no answer."

"I spoke with Tolkien briefly this morning," Fleming said. "He was on his way to see Mr. Loening to talk about his book."

"*The Hobbit.*"

"Have you read it?"

"No."

"Why is it so popular here, do you know?"

"They think the dragon is England, hording the world's wealth while others starve."

Fleming took a moment to look around at the throngs of Berliners going about their day. Well-dressed, well-fed, high color. *Starving?* Not quite. He had not read *The Hobbit* either, but he had been briefed on it, and on its author, by his contact at MI-6. Tolkien may be unwittingly helping the Nazis by having his book published in German, but he had agreed without hesitation to lend a hand in the mission now under way. Untrained, living in an ivory tower at Oxford, he could easily be killed. That took pluck. The dragon indeed. He decided not to comment, to change the subject.

"Who was that young chap," he asked, "who joined you after I departed Tuesday evening?"

"Kurt? A college friend from Heidelberg, where my father taught."

Fleming paused to sip his coffee.

"*He's* a Nazi, no doubt."

"He thinks he is."

Now the Englishman screwed up his face, trying for comically quizzical, remembering Kurt, tall and blond and rigid, in his SS uniform, standing next to Billie at the Sportpalast last week. *Thinks* he is?

"He was a charming boy from the country when I first met him," Billie said, smiling wryly.

"His heart is good, you mean."

"Yes. I've invited him to stop by this afternoon."

"He's SS. But you know that of course."

"You must trust me, Ian. He's just a boy, and he may be more helpful than you imagine."

More helpful with what? Fleming said to himself, but decided to let this pass as well. *Ian, that sounded nice.*

"Should I be jealous?" he asked.

"Is that why you were spying on me?"

"Well, if you must know . . ."

"He's just an old friend."

"And me?"

"You are a new friend."

"*Is* there someone special, Billie?"

"No. But Ian . . . you will be going home soon. And there will be war. Unless . . ."

"Unless what?"

Billie paused, and Fleming could see she was trying to decide whether to tell him something or not. She had mentioned a secret passion. It certainly wasn't apple strudel or alpine hiking. Nor was it sexual. He was not an idiot. *Tell me, Billie for Lillian*—a shared secret at this stage, well, it would be a delicious thing.

"Take me to dinner tonight," Billie said. "We will talk."

"I will, gladly," Fleming replied. "By the way, what is Kurt's surname?"

"It's Bauer, but why do you ask?"

Ah, the farmer, the Englishman said to himself, *the yokel.* He was looking into the café's broad front window at the reflection of Kurt Bauer standing nonchalantly at a tram stop on the far corner of Unter den Linden, concentrating on a folded newspaper as if it meant his very life to him, in mufti now, a fedora pulled down almost to his eyes. *No white smock and straw hat now, I see.*

"No reason," Fleming answered. "I just like to know who my rivals are."

"He's not a rival," Billie said, smiling her dazzling smile. "But you may believe what you wish. A bit of jealousy is endearing to a woman. But just a bit."

"Then," said Fleming, returning her smile with a sly one of his own, out of the corner of his eye watching Bauer get on the bright yellow tram, "I shall be just a bit jealous and no more. We Englishmen are nothing if not understated."

9.

Berlin
October 6, 1938, 2:00 p.m.

Reinhard Heydrich was in the midst of planning something far more important than the pursuit of Himmler's foolish dream of discovering the ultimate weapon in an ancient spell or trinket. He had been tasked by Hitler himself with finding and implementing the most efficient means of ridding Germany, once and for all, of its biggest problem, its Jews. This final solution, this *Endlosung*, he had pursued with relish. *This* would be a historic achievement. Indeed, his next appointment was to be with his old Reichsmarine colleague, Walter Rauff, who had invented something intriguing he called a mobile gas chamber. And Standartenfuhrer Rauff was helping him plan an operation that, one night soon, would soon mark the beginning of the *Endlosung*.

Still, Himmler was not someone to be disobeyed or taken lightly. He controlled all of the SS and its sub-units, the SD, the Orpo, the Kripo, the Gestapo, the fledgling Waffen-SS. As to the Jews, Himmler hated them even more than Hitler. Indeed, Himmler had built the first of the concentration camps, at Dachau, and had personally designed the death's head insignia for the guards' uniforms. Himmler had *made* Heydrich, with the Fuhrer's full support, and so many fanatically loyal followers; he could unmake him overnight. Thus the need for the meeting that had just ended with Lazarus, his mole in Operation Odin. Glancing first at his watch—he had ten minutes—and then at the agent's neatly typed two-page report, Gruppenfuhrer Heydrich recalled their conversation.

> Lazarus: I have always thought this visit was a bad idea. The reporter, Fleming, I think he was spying in Moscow at the Vickers trial. He is MI-6.
>
> Heydrich: I told you, Goebbels wants it. Do not raise this point again. Just do your job. What has Fleming been up to?
>
> Lazarus: Nothing. As you have seen in my report, coffee on Unter den Linden this morning. He interviews the two professors today at 3:00 p.m.
>
> Heydrich: You will be there?
>
> Lazarus: Of course.
>
> Heydrich: Recording?
>
> Lazarus: Yes, the construction is perfect cover for our people.
>
> Heydrich: I see that Shroeder and Tolkien met last night, but you were unable to record.

Lazarus: Yes, unfortunately.

Heydrich: Why not.

Lazarus: There was music playing.

Heydrich: Had you not accounted for that?

Lazarus: The Victrola has always been in the parlor. Shroeder must have brought it into his study for Tolkien's visit. He must have placed it very near the microphone.

Heydrich: What was the music?

Lazarus: *Gotterdammerung.*

Heydrich: And Tolkien? Is he the fool we think he is? This silly book.

Lazarus: Dr. Goebbels says it has propaganda value.

Heydrich: When does Tolkien leave?

Lazarus: He has a five-day visa. The interviews are this afternoon, with film. Tomorrow, some additional footage in Berlin. *The professors visit the Altes. Etcetera.*

Heydrich: More nonsense.

Lazarus: Tolkien leaves on Monday.

Heydrich: As soon as he leaves, I want a demonstration.

Lazarus: Shroeder says he needs the amulet.

Heydrich: *Says?*

Lazarus: Yes, I believe he has it.

Heydrich: You *believe* he has it.

Lazarus: Yes, I believe he has it hidden somewhere in his apartment.

Heydrich: Have you searched the apartment?

Lazarus: Shroeder and Tolkien are going out to dinner tonight. We will search then.

Heydrich: Good. If you find it, we will know that Shroeder has been playing us for fools.

Lazarus: He will say it's not the right one. He will have an excuse.

Heydrich: Tell him that nevertheless we insist on a demonstration. On Monday.

Lazarus: If he refuses?

Heydrich: He will not refuse.

Lazarus: He may rather die.

Heydrich: He will not refuse.

Lazarus: Shall we film it? Perhaps
Frau Reifensthal?

Heydrich: Yes. Please arrange it.

Heydrich's secretary was knocking at his door, no
doubt to announce Walter Rauff. The Gestapo chief
slid the report into its Top Secret folder and opened a
desk drawer to put it away, smiling as he remembered
the brief quizzical look on his mole's face when he
said "*he will not refuse*" for the second time.

10.
Berlin
October 6, 1938, 6:00 p.m.

"Shall we walk?" Billie Shroeder said, taking Ian Fleming's arm. "The Tiergarten is beautiful at this time of year."

"Of course, it's a lovely evening."

They crossed Hermann Goering Strasse and entered the huge urban park under a filigreed wrought iron arch that reminded Fleming of the entrances to the Jardin Anglais in Geneva, where he had studied and had briefly been engaged to be married.

"So, how did it go?" Billie said.

"The old gents?" Fleming replied. "Topping. You were there."

"They seemed quite relaxed and comfortable, smiling and discussing all of those old Norse gods," Billie said. "But it's your eye that matters, not mine."

"And Kurt Bauer's. He seemed very much in control."

"The project is very important, and he is answerable to Goebbels."

"I thought Himmler was Kurt's boss, the SS."

"I suppose he is on loan. I confuse these giants of the Reich. Don't be so hard on Kurt. He is just doing his job."

"Billie . . ."

"Yes?"

"Nothing."

Billie squeezed his arm. *Thanking me,* Fleming thought, *for laying off Bauer, her college chum with the good heart.*

"Why is this called the Animal Garden?" Fleming asked.

They were strolling easily under an awning of tall gold-and-red-leafed branches, the trees lining both sides of the cinder path stately, well-kept maples and oaks in their full autumn glory. The last of the day's brilliant sunshine was at their backs, casting long shadows of their bodies. *On stilts,* Fleming thought, enjoying the touch of Billie's hand on his bicep. *Still in shape,* he thought, *thank God, all that MI-6 training, worse than Eton and that bloody scrumming about.*

"It was a private hunting ground at one time," Billie said. "A few hundred years ago. There is still a zoo."

"Ah yes, medieval Europe. The good old days. *Le droite du seigneur,* by God."

"Ian." Another squeeze of the arm and a smile.

"Of course the war ended all that, not that it ever mattered much to me. My brother inherits."

"*Ian.*"

"Joking old girl,"

"I'm quite relieved."

"Shall we sit," Fleming said. They were approaching a small lake, ringed by trees, with benches very close to its edge. They walked in silence and, once seated, Billie moved close and again took Fleming's arm.

"Don't be offended, Herr Fleming," Billie said, "but you are not married, are you?"

"Of course not, heaven forbid."

"Ah, heaven forbid . . ."

Billie looked away, at the fiery reflection of the trees on the flat lake surface.

"I suppose I should not have invoked heaven."

"It's just an expression," Billie said. "Still, it is *heaven* that sanctions marriage, don't you think?"

"I've never thought of it quite that way, but you may be right."

"My father says your family is quite important."

"Not true."

"That your father died in the war."

"True."

"How old were you?"

"Nine."

"And now?"

"Thirty."

"Please forgive the inquisition, but . . ."

"But what?"

"You seem not determined to bed me, unlike so many men I meet nowadays."

Breathing room, Fleming thought, a strategy that had become natural to him when it came to certain women.

"You're a sweet girl, Billie. Fire away." Fleming reached across his chest and covered Billie's hand with his as he said this.

"No more questions. But you may ask *me.*"

You're not a virgin, I hope, Fleming thought, suddenly nervous.

They were silent for a moment, then Billie said, "I see. I have a *little* experience, but not much." Fleming, taken aback, turned to look at Billie, who smiled at him, then put her head on his shoulder. Her silky dark brown hair smelled faintly of gardenia, or perhaps jasmine, transporting him for a moment from the marshal atmosphere of Berlin, from the winter and the war that was about to descend on Europe, to a place he could not name. Europe-bound, it was his first heady whiff of the tropics, a world he had not yet experienced.

"Your hair, it smells lovely," Fleming said.

Something about Billie's reply, a barely audible murmur, touched the Englishman's heart. He pulled away slightly and with his free hand lifted Billie's face gently by the chin so that they were looking into each other's eyes. *Damn,* he thought, *bloody hell.*

"Shall we get back?" Billie said. "Perhaps we can have a drink in my room before dinner."

11.
Berlin
October 6, 1938, 7:00 p.m.

Draco sit meus dux,
Crux non sit mea lux,
Satana, aggredere,
Mihi da quod rogo,
Quod mihi offert bonum est,
Bibam laete toxicum.

"Franz, I'm at a loss," said Tolkien, "this seems to be an invocation to the devil." He was holding a letter-sized piece of parchment that was under glass in a simple wooden frame.

"It is. Shall I translate it for you?"

"Please."

"*Let the dragon be my guide. Let not the cross be my light. Step forward Satan. Give me what I ask. What you offer me is good. I will gladly drink the poison.*"

"Is it . . . is it the reverse of the *Vedo Retro Satana*? Can it be?"

"It is."

The two dons were standing at the waist-high parapet on the roof of Franz Shroeder's apartment building. Below them the lights of the vast seven-hundred-year-old city were beginning to come on, at first one by one, then in small numbers, then in swaths that finally stretched from the city center to its encircling suburbs.

The forest and farmland beyond the perimeter of this brightly lit grid were doing the opposite, going from pearly gray to pitch black before their eyes. To their left, not far from central Berlin, planes were landing and taking off at Templehof Airport, some entering and emerging from the completed section of the huge, curved main terminal complex that was under construction day and night. Unter den Linden, Freidrichstrasse, the King's Highway, Wilhelmstrasse and the other main avenues of the metropolis were lit by moving automobile headlights and stately gas streetlights, some of them over a century old, curving away into the distance. The new chancellery and other government buildings, all draped in blood-red Nazi banners, were floodlit from above and below. Hitler's *Germania* lay spread out before them. It looked every bit the world capital he envisioned it to be.

"It's made from wolf skin," Shroeder said.

"Wolf skin?"

"Yes, circa 1400. I had it analyzed."

"Father Adelbert's incantation."

"Yes. I should have told you sooner. I've performed the ritual. It works."

"You mean . . . ?"

"Yes. When Billie was five, she had a cat that was dying. I brought it to Deggendorf. It died on the train. On that day in 1872, after taking the amulet and the parchment from Father Adelbert, I found the tunnel he used and used it to escape. I marked the entrance in my mind's eye—it was on a hill behind the old Roman wall near the abbey orchard—and easily found it again. Everything was the same, the altar, the giant tree, except now the saplings were gone. Immediately, I performed the ritual, the cat jumped up and bounded off. I was stunned, as you can imagine. The air was suddenly thick and sulfurous. Until that day, my hair was brown. Frightened, I raced to the tunnel. Climbing up to the ledge to get to it, my foot got stuck between two boulders. I wrenched it free in my panic and damaged the ankle irreparably."

"But you lived. Brother Adelbert died."

"He died the *second* time he did it."

"Franz . . ."

"When everyone was leaving this afternoon, Kurt Bauer pulled me aside. He told me that they were aborting the Externsteine expedition. Himmler wants a demonstration from me on Monday, as soon as you've left. He has a Nazi smile, young Kurt, a wicked smile. He seems to know, somehow, that the ritual will work."

"Does Bauer know about the parchment?"

"Yes, I've shown it to him. I felt I had to show him a sign of progress."

"And the amulet?"

"I've led him on several wild goose chases. But now I fear he knows I have it."

"Do you think he knows about your hiding place?"

"I think he does, I fear that all of my movements are being watched. I sense a darkness, a coldness near me and around me all the time. I have removed the amulet and re-hidden it."

Tolkien remained silent, recalling the chill in Shroeder's study last night, the far-off look in the German professor's eyes as he gazed at the fire, as if he were looking into an unhappy future, or a bizarre new world.

"I thought Bauer was a friend of your daughter's?"

"He is a Nazi of the most vicious kind."

"Then why . . . ?"

"She is blinded by friendship. They are college chums."

"Or love perhaps."

"God forbid."

"Franz, if they are going to harm you, you can flee. I will help you."

The old man's smile was big and toothy, but rueful. "It is not me I care about, my life is over. It's Billie. It is *her* life that is at stake."

Professor Tolkien had written fiction. He knew that conflict was essential to a good story, that the more intense was the conflict, the more gripping would be the tale. But now here was real life. Billie Shroeder would die if Franz did not produce what Himmler wanted. But what Himmler wanted was an evil thing, likely to doom the human race.

"I do not sleep well," Shroeder said.

"I do not doubt it."

"I come up here at dawn sometimes. The sunrise is beautiful, wondrous, over the city. I forget for a few moments about the evil that is gripping my country, my beloved Germany."

They gazed at the city in silence.

"I will take the figurine with me to England," Tolkien said at length. "Separate it from the amulet."

"No, my dear John, that would only delay the final dawn."

"The final dawn?"

"The parchment and the figurine must be destroyed together. If they are not, there will soon be no more dawns for Berlin, no more dawns for men."

"I will help you."

"No, you must return to your wife and children."

Tolkien did not reply. A few moments ago, at the horizon, the top rim of the setting sun had flashed elliptically for an instant between the rim of the earth below and a line of fiery red clouds above, a fierce, bloody eye looking pitilessly upon the world of men. The night was normal now, like any other mild autumn night. But that eye at the horizon, had it looked right at him? Into his soul? Edith, young John, Michael, Christopher, Priscilla: *you must never see that eye.*

12.
Berlin
October 6, 1938, 8:00 p.m.

"We haven't had a chance to talk."

"No."

"Dicey, all this spying. A bit steep for a banker and a university don."

"I thought you were a reporter."

"Only occasionally. The bank gives me leave."

"Do you like beer?"

"*Bier gut.*"

Tolkien smiled. "Let's pop in here then."

They passed through an arched entryway into a large garden adjacent to a restaurant. A dozen or so vending tents with beer insignia on their sides lined the garden's perimeter. In front of each tent stood rows of picnic tables filled with Berliners laughing, gesturing, talking, some singing, all enjoying foamy-headed German lager from large ceramic steins. In the center a noisy carousel—a menagerie of brightly painted horses, unicorns, and African animals—rotated slowly, its organ blaring a polka. Some of the people waiting for their turn on the carousel were dancing. The lights from the vending tents and the carousel lit the whole garden.

"You must find a seat where you can," a buxom blond waitress in a dirndl, her breasts trying hard to break free from her ruffled white blouse, said to them in German. She was holding three full beer steins in each hand, smiling happily.

"*Danke*," Tolkien and Fleming said in unison.

They found an empty table for four in a corner on the far side of the carousel. Another buxom, smiling waitress, this one brunette, brought them a pitcher and two glasses and left. They realized they were supposed to fill the pitcher at the vending tent of their choice. While Fleming went off to do this, Professor Tolkien lit his pipe and looked around. In the short few days since Arlie Cavanaugh had recruited him for this mission, he had been reading all he could about the current state of world affairs. He was a quick study, but nothing he had read had prepared him for the conclusion he reached after observing the people of Berlin for only two days. On the streets, on the trolleys, in the shops, in the restaurants, he saw it everywhere: the German people had sold their collective soul to the devil. Behind the smugness, the arrogance of easy victories, the contempt for the weakness of France and England, he saw not the slightest trace of bravado. They believed they were superior, above morality. They had abandoned the thing that made them human.

"So," Fleming said, after returning and filling their glasses. "How did it go with Loening?"

"I turned him down."

"Turned him down? Why?"

"He wanted me to sign an oath saying I wasn't a Jew."

"Ah, the Nuremberg Laws."

"What are *they*?"

"You can't marry a Jew, etcetera. Legalized discrimination."

"I'm not marrying a Jew. I'm married."

"The German bureaucrats are worse than the Soviets. They salivate over repressive laws. The Jews are allowed to breathe German air, but only until a way can be found to round them all up and kill them. Until then they will be harassed and tortured and killed off a few at a time, like rats. '*Judenrein*,' the Nazi's call it. Jew-free."

"I daresay . . ."

"Yes?"

"There are too many."

"That's what Hitler says."

Tolkien looked at Fleming and then at the crowd of Germans—mostly young but many older—laughing, smiling, dancing, their eyes made bright by alcohol and pride. And power and revenge. How many Jews were there in Germany? In Europe? He placed his hand on his shirt front and felt the outline of the St. Benedict medal he had worn since returning home from the war, the one he had purchased in Calais before boarding the hospital ship that would take him back to England, a hasty replacement for the one that Edith had given him the night before he shipped out. *Get thee back Satan,* he whispered to himself.

"Are you there, Professor?" Fleming said.

"Yes."

"Good, we must work. You used the code for urgent."

"Yes."

"Go on."

"Professor Shroeder has told me what he's working on."

Fleming smiled. "It's simple, this spying business, no?"

"In this case, yes. And no."

* * *

"Professor Tolkien, I'm not often at a loss for words."

"But you are now."

"Not quite." Nevertheless, Fleming said nothing. The facts of the matter had taken Tolkien only a few minutes to narrate. The sinking in was the hard part.

"You are skeptical," the professor said.

Fleming did not reply.

"A cynic."

"I'm both," Fleming said. "Do you believe Shroeder? When he says he raised the dead cat?"

"Yes, I do."

"Bloody hell."

"I haven't told you everything. Billie Shroeder will be killed if Franz does not perform the ritual on Monday. Franz has asked me to help get her out of Germany."

"What did you say?"

"I said I would."

"What do you have in mind? A boat ride down the Rhine? They'll never let her out."

"I thought I'd ask you."

"Bloody hell."

"My sentiments."

"You'll all have to leave."

"All?"

"You, Shroeder, and Billie."

"Before Monday, you mean?"

"Yes."

"But I can leave on Monday by myself. I have my plane ticket."

"I can't leave you behind. You'll be arrested once they realize that Shroeder and Billie are missing. You are in Nazi Germany, professor, the epicenter of evil on Earth. They will crucify you."

"And where do you think this evil comes from?"

"Pardon?"

"Where does this evil come from?"

"Hitler, Goebbels, Goering, the lot of them."

"Who put it in them?"

"My dear chap . . ."

"I'm not your dear chap, Fleming. I'm your elder by sixteen years. I fought the Hun in France. I have asked myself since, how did that war happen, how and why does evil exist?"

"Did you come up with an answer?"

"No. But I will tell you this, after all the thought I've given it: the raising of the dead does not seem so farfetched given the evil spell that seems to have been cast on mankind from its very beginnings."

Fleming smiled and leaned back in his chair. Leaning forward again, he lifted the pitcher and topped off their glasses. "I apologize," he said.

"For what?"

"For condescending to you. You are far above me in all ways."

"You are mistaken. You are upper crust. I am low born. I've meant to ask you, was your father Valentine Fleming?"

"Yes."

"I met him once. He gave me a letter to send to your mother, which I did when I read Churchill's eulogy in the *Times*."

Fleming was almost instantly taken back to June of 1917, to the scene in the "large" drawing room (as opposed to the many smaller ones) at Joyce Grove, his grandfather's sprawling, rather brutal-looking manor house in Oxfordshire that was his second home growing up. His mother, in black from head to toe, bereft of her usual brilliant jewelry, her face white but composed, had stood in front of the room's cavernous fireplace and read the letter to him and his three brothers, whose nannies had been told to dress them for the occasion. He was nine at the time. If she had mentioned the name of the soldier who had sent it, Fleming had long forgotten it. But he did remember one line: remind the children that if another war comes, they must do their duty.

First metaphysics and now this, Fleming thought. *Who is this fellow Tolkien?* "You met my father?" he said.

"Yes. In the war."

"But . . . How? When?"

"I'll tell you another time. There is other, more pressing business now."

Fleming did not respond. He had few solid memories of his father, the great, heroic Val Fleming, made immortal by Churchill, but those he did have he had enshrined in a compartment in his mind that was like a church, so sacred were its precincts. He longed to add to this small trove. Instinctively, he put his hand inside his jacket and ran his fingers along the outline of his wallet, which contained his most treasured possession, given to him by his mother that day at Joyce Grove.

"I promise," Tolkien said, interrupting Fleming's thoughts. "But now tell me, what are your plans?"

Fleming again fell silent. *This is for Johnny,* his mother had said. A line on a piece of paper and an artifact, they were all Ian Fleming had of Val Fleming. He had clung all the harder to these things as the few memories he had of the man faded with the years. *I'll tell you another time, I promise,* Tolkien had said, as if he were speaking to a schoolboy. *No, don't beg old man,* Fleming said to himself. *Old Tolkien means no harm. He'll tell you one day soon.*

"Fleming," said Tolkien.

"I'm going to contact Bletchley," Fleming replied, wrenching himself from his private thoughts, "to recommend immediate extraction."

"How long will that take."

"I will emphasize the urgency of the situation."

"What shall I tell professor Shroeder?"

"Tell him nothing until I contact you with Bletchley's answer. But keep him close. I believe we will be traveling on a moment's notice."

"And Miss Shroeder?"

"I will take care of her. And by the way, Professor, I will be extracting the amulet and the parchment as well. If there is anything to this raising-the-dead business, it is the British who will take advantage of it. No one else."

13.
Berlin
October 6, 1938, 11:30 p.m.

"When did you first come to Berlin, Ian?"

"I stopped here in 1933 on my way home from Moscow. Hitler had just been named chancellor."

"Why were you in Moscow?"

"Covering a trial for *Reuters*."

"You were quite young, no?"

"Twenty-five."

"What trial? I was at school then and not political at all."

"Some Brits were accused of being spies."

"How exciting."

"Not for them."

"How did you find Berlin?"

"Sickening. Hitler's police state had begun."

Fleming and Billie were walking along Unter den Linden, heading back to the Adlon after a quiet dinner at a small café tucked in a side street off of Freidrichstrasse. It was raining when they emerged from the restaurant, and the street and sidewalks were glistening from the pale yellow reflection of the gas lamps that lit their way. Auto and foot traffic was light, the rain having driven people inside and quieted this normally bustling part of the city. Fleming, in a dark blue suit, white dress shirt, and light blue striped bowtie, had brought an umbrella. Billie, at

Fleming's insistence, was wearing his black fedora, her highly impractical velvet pillbox hat in her coat pocket. Arm-in-arm, they were cozy under the umbrella, minding little when a sideways breeze would blow some rainwater against them.

Billie remained silent. They were walking under the densely leafed trees that gave the famous boulevard its name. At dinner she had told Fleming about her quiet, motherless childhood in Heidelberg, her uneventful college years, her devotion to her father. How did such a beautiful flower emerge from that desert? Under an especially thickly leafed tree, he brought them to a halt, and swung her gently around to face him. The occasional drop of rain that reached them pinged against the umbrella, heightening, or so it seemed to Fleming, the sense that he and Billie were a solitary pair, alone, cut off in the dark and the rain from the world's madness.

"You never told me your secret," he said.

"Ah, yes." Billie had to tilt the fedora back on her head in order to look up and see him. "My secret."

"Your secret passion."

"I was half-hoping you wouldn't ask and half-hoping you would."

"I'm asking."

"I have joined a small resistance group. At least I think it's small. How many cells there are, I do not know."

Resistance? Cells?

"I have compromised you. I'm sorry, but there is no one else I can talk to. I have felt so alone and my father, well, he is a dreamer."

"Billie."

"Yes."

They were standing very close to each other now, their arms, except for Fleming's umbrella arm, at their sides.

"Yes, Ian."

"What is your cell up to?"

"We arrange to get Jews out of Germany. The ones who can't afford the exit fees."

"Which is most of them."

"Yes, they are countless."

"How?"

"There is an underground, mostly at the Dutch border. We buy British immigration commissions. They're very expensive. We try to forge them. Ian?"

"Yes?"

"I have another reason for telling you."

"Yes?"

"We need your help."

"Who is we?"

"You must realize I can't tell you that."

"My help?"

"Yes, bringing someone out. We need your connections."

"I have no connections."

Silence. Her large, liquid eyes looking up into his. Gritty, brave, imploring. Who is this woman?

"Who is it?" he asked.

"Someone your government would be interested in talking to, an engineer. He is working on a coating for tanks that would repel magnetic mines."

"His name?"

"I don't know."

"Where is he?"

"He works for Krupp in Magdaberg."

"He wants to defect?"

"Yes. He's a Jew, but that the Nazis do not know. If they find out he will be killed."

At dinner, he had told Billie about his meeting with Professor Tolkien and of his encounter with the Nuremberg laws. She applauded the English don's courage. Had she known that in one day he had uncovered the truth about her father's work for Himmler, she would have been more impressed. But that information he could not reveal, not yet. Billie and her father were in grave danger, but he could do nothing to help them until he communicated with Bletchley House.

14.

Berlin
October 7, 1938, 1:00 a.m.

"*Guten abend,* Herr Fleming. Will you have your customary nightcap?"

"No, Hans, I'm not well tonight."

"Baking soda, perhaps?"

"Yes, please."

"Shall I send it to your room?"

"That would be best."

Hans, the bartender at the Adlon was a Nazi-hater who had lost an eye in France in the war. His patch did not quite cover the scar tissue, but no one dared look too closely, nor did any of the SS and Gestapo officers who stopped on a regular basis to check on the doings of the foreigners at the popular hotel ever think about questioning his loyalty. He was short and stocky and had an angry cross-hatched scar on the cheek under his bad eye, but in his maroon vest, snow-white shirt, and black bowtie he exuded a menacing sort of dignity, not unlike the butlers who ran the Fleming homes in Oxfordshire and Grosvenor Square with white-gloved iron fists.

This was the first time that Fleming had used the baking soda bit, but it worked like a charm. The waiter who brought it up was Hans' brother, also a veteran, also versed in precisely what to say. Fleming gave him a 5-Reichsmark coin as a tip, one of the recently issued ones with the Nazi eagle and swastika on one side and Von Hindenburg in profile on the other. In the center of the old field marshal's ear was a microdot with virtually the same shiny silver surface as the newly minted coin.

When the waiter left, Fleming poured cold water from the silver carafe and mixed in the white powder. He was not sick, and Billie, asleep in his bed, was not looking, but he had been taught to follow through, to act always as if someone *was* looking. Taste the fucking baking soda, one of his several trainers had said, swallow it, apropos of the very drill he and Hans and his brother had just meticulously carried out. He finished the drink, then dipped the end of a linen napkin into the iced water. Slipping into bed, he propped himself on an elbow and patted the wet napkin on Billie's forehead until her eyes came open and she smiled.

"Was I asleep?"

"Yes. I'm afraid I fed you too much champagne."

"What time is it?"

"Oneish."

"What? I slept for two hours?"

"Just under."

"I'm foggy . . ."

"You look ravishing."

Now Billie noticed that she had on one of Fleming's pajama tops, creamy white with black piping at the cuffs and *ILF* embroidered in black on the pocket.

"Ian . . . ?"

"No."

"No, what?"

"No, nothing happened. You were legless. I sent you to the loo to change. Now here we are."

"What have you been doing?"

"Spy stuff."

"What?"

"I'm a spy. I've been writing a message in code, then creating a microdot, which I've sent by courier pigeon to London."

"My hero, so brave, so dashing."

71

"A hell of a thing, trapping that pigeon and training it while you slept."

"Certainly not beyond you."

"Certainly not."

"Are you sure you didn't drug me? Get me out of the way? I had the strangest dreams."

"What kind of dreams?"

"Lightning bolts in the room, several flashes of it, and men's voices at the end of a long tunnel."

"So it worked."

"Worked?"

"The Mickey Finn I gave you. That's what the Americans call it."

"Hmmm . . ."

"It's also a love potion."

Fleming, smiling, ran his fingers along Billie's brow.

"Hmmm . . ."

"How does it work?"

"A deep sleep, then one long kiss, and then it's activated."

"I'm feeling something already," Billie said, looking into Fleming's eyes, smiling herself now.

"That's . . . well, that's *me*," Fleming said. In his pajama bottoms, he had kicked off his slippers and loosened his wing-collar shirt before lifting the coverlet and sliding in next to Billie. On his right side, he was now leaning gently into her left flank.

"I see, that *is* you," Billie said.

"Shall we activate the potion?"

"Before we do, will you help me?"

"With your engineer, you mean?"

"Yes."

"I'll do what I can."

"Promise?"

"Yes."

"It's not your gentleman friend I feel against my leg talking?"

"No."

"There's no need to activate the potion, as you say, but yes, please do."

<u>15.</u>
Berlin
October 7, 1938, 7:00 a.m.

"How far down is it, do you think?" Trygg Korumak asked.

"Perhaps thirty meters," Professor Tolkien replied. "Don't look."

"I thought your people have lived in the mountains for generations," said Professor Shroeder.

"Yes," Korumak answered, "*in* them, not *on* them."

"Ah, another of your riddles."

"What riddles?" Tolkien asked.

"Trygg himself is a riddle," the German professor said, flashing a quick, wry smile. "A riddle who lives *in* mountains but not on them and is afraid of heights."

"Perhaps this is a bad idea," Tolkien said.

They were standing at the northern parapet on the roof of Professor Shroeder's apartment building. At their backs, dawn was spreading its pink and gray glow over Berlin. Before them, across a fifteen-foot chasm, was the roof of the building next door. Seven stories below was the cement floor of the courtyard between the two buildings. A ladder lay across the chasm.

"This thing looked sturdy before we laid it down," said Korumak, whose normally ruddy cheeks were now a pale white. "It looks like a toothpick now."

"It's our only chance," said Shroeder.

"Perhaps the next building will not be so far away," said Tolkien.

Earlier, at the west parapet, they had peered down and seen the Daimler parked in the small field at the rear of the building. At the curb in front was another Daimler, this one with a soldier in SS gray standing next to it drinking from a tin mug. Korumak, whose weakness was heights, but who apparently had many talents, had found the apartment's hidden microphones and connected their input wires to the building's doorbell system, which meant that whoever was listening would hear nothing but the occasional bell ringing. How much time that would buy them, they did not know. They assumed not much. They had dared not try the loud music trick again. At seven in the morning, and with all five microphones emitting only Wagner or something similar, they would have quickly been discovered.

"I'll go first," said Tolkien, when he realized that Shroeder and Korumak were staring at him intently, their mouths shut, waiting for him to continue. *To lead them*, he thought. "I'll anchor the ladder on the other side. We did similar exercises during the war. It's not so hard." He spoke briskly, without hesitation, trying to exude a confidence he did not feel. He had seen the old wooden ladder sticking out from a paint-stained canvas tarp when he and Shroeder had met on the roof the evening before. Remembering the scaling and rappelling training he had done on Cannock Chase in Staffordshire, he had been the one to suggest escaping across Hermann Goering Strasse's rooftops. *Of course I was twenty-three then*, he now said to himself.

"We need you, Trygg," said Shroeder.

It was Trygg who had said that stealing a car would be easy, that most people left the key in the ignition when they parked their car, and that he could easily power the ignition without a key if necessary. They would head north, he said, in the opposite direction of Deggendorf. No one would be looking for them north of Berlin. He knew a place where they could cross quietly into Poland and from there travel south until they had to cross back again into Germany near Metten Abbey. A seven-hundred-ki-lometer journey, and fraught with danger, but he had friends, the little man had said, who would help them along the way. Who was this dwarf? Who were these friends? Were they a ring of car thieves? How did he know so much about electrical engineering? Tolk-ien felt sorry for the dwarf, who, with his bowlegs and low center of gravity, was clearly not built for gymnastics. Far from it. A fall from the ladder meant certain death. But yes, Professor Shroeder was right, they needed Korumak, they needed him badly, and for reasons that seemed both clouded in mystery and yet vitally important.

"These things are weighing heavily," Shroeder said, brushing his fingers on his sternum. He had the amulet on a silver chain around his neck and the parchment sewn into the lining of his tweed jacket.

Hearing this, Professor Tolkien lifted the sack they had carried up with them containing the two sofa pillows that Trygg would sit on while driving, and flung it across the chasm to the roof opposite, where it landed with a quiet thud. Then, whispering to himself, *hand-foot, hand-foot*, he knelt on the para-pet and started across.

16.
Berlin
October 7, 1938, 11:00 a.m.

Ian Fleming stood inside the front door of the Olympic Boxing Club, unfolding his umbrella, his dripping Macintosh forming puddles at his feet. He was astonished at the size of the crowd sitting on rows of benches around the center ring. One of them, front row center, he recognized as a German movie star, now brunette, but a sexy, flirtatious blond in a Hitchcock movie he had seen a dozen or so years ago in Geneva. She was smoking a cigarette in an ivory holder and chatting with a middle-aged man in a dark suit and tie sitting next to her, leaning close to the man's ear, so as, Fleming assumed, to be heard over the general din. In the movie, she had killed Cyril Richard who had tried to rape her. With a knife. What was her name?

Hanging from the twenty-foot-high ceiling were a series of sweating, rusting parallel pipes that branched out in the middle diagonally like a metro map. Naked light bulbs hanging in wire cages lit the room, mostly illuminating the smoke from a hundred cigarettes. Leather punching bags, some for hand work, some for body work, hung from steel braces in each of the room's four corners. A group of men, reporters he recognized, were gathered around a scale on a pedestal on the right wall, taking turns weighing themselves, joking, passing around a flask. *The press,* Fleming thought, *my kind of people.*

"That's Anny Ondra," said a voice behind him. "Schmeling's wife."

Fleming turned to see Rex Dowling, the American reporter, grinning at him, his straw-blond hair a dull brown now, and plastered to his head, a handkerchief raised to mop the rain from his face.

"I see you don't believe in umbrellas."

"They're for sissies."

Fleming smiled. He and Dowling had been playing an unacknowledged game, the English toff versus the American hayseed, since they first covered the Berlin Olympics together in 1936. "They don't get pneumonia though," he replied.

Dowling smiled his big, dumb, handsome smile and shrugged, saying through his teeth, "I have a message for you."

"From whom?" The even pitch of the Englishman's voice hid his inner concern. Dowling had also spotted Billie at the Sportpalast last week. He also stayed at the Adlon. And he had bedded half the women in the place, or so it was said.

"Your Uncle Quex."

Fleming remained silent, absorbing this entirely unexpected answer.

"He says the sun is shining in Hyde Park."

"That's rare this time of year."

"No need for an umbrella."

Fleming now quickly eyed Dowling from head to toe. "Shall we sit," he said. "I see two empty seats in the last row, there, near those bags."

After they were seated, both men took out notepads and pencils. They both knew that they actually had to file stories on what had been touted as Max Schmeling's first open-to-the-public appearance in a ring since his devastating loss to Joe Louis, the great American "Braun Bomber," in June. He was to spar with the German amateur heavyweight champ, a young, sculpted-from-marble Aryan named Bruno

Schmidt, whom the boxing-mad German people had taken to their bosom after Max's debacle in New York. Though it was billed as a simple spar, the rumor had been spreading that Schmidt was going to fight for real, perhaps to knock the disgraced Schmeling out. Thus the large crowd of reporters, politicians, and in-favor celebrities in the room. Goebbels, who had loved Schmeling after he beat Louis in 1936, now hated him. The man had never joined the Nazi Party. His manager was a Jew. The sycophantic German *haute monde* crowd naturally followed suit. It had just been announced that the handsome but now former world champion would be fighting Adolf Heuser next year for the European Heavyweight title. No one cared. They wanted to see him pummeled, toppled once and for all from Germany's boxing pinnacle.

"What's the message?" Fleming asked.

"You need to extract three people."

"Yes. By Sunday."

"There is a farm in Meppen, on the Muhlenberg road, near the Dutch border. A kilometer after an abandoned rail spur, on the right. The farmhouse is right on the road. Two yellow lights will be on above the front door. Your plane will land between ten and midnight. The pilot will only wait five minutes. You are to board as well."

"Thank you."

"You are to ask for Baron Rilke. 'I am here to call on Baron Rilke. Baron Maximilian Rilke? No, Baron Laurens Rilke.' If the two lights are not on, do not turn in. You are to contact your embassy about getting up to Meppen. It's a haul."

"How do I contact you? In an emergency, I mean."

"Tell Hans you are looking for the handsome American from Chicago."

"And you'll appear."

"Or someone in my place. He or she will want to know what time it is London."

"Simple."

"Yes."

"Thank you again."

"Good luck."

Fleming did not answer. Schmidt and Schmeling had entered the ring, both wearing headgear. He eyed Schmeling—six foot tall, heavy browed, perhaps a hundred ninety pounds, thirty-two inch waist, muscular but slim for a heavyweight. He was bouncing on his toes, staying warm. Schmidt was perhaps two-ten, all muscle, but a lumberer, easily out-maneuvered. It occurred to Fleming that Schmeling could kill Schmidt if he wanted to. Send him to the Norse version of Hades. He remembered what his boxing instructor at Bletchley, a gnarled, retired middleweight from the East End, his cockney accent thick and garbled, had told him: it's the element of surprise, milord. You're bound to get into a scuffle or two. Don't waste time. A right to the bridge of the nose will kill a man just as soon as one of them fancy karate chops or judo kicks. Karate he had pronounced *karayty*, judo *jew*-dough, like Cary Grant's *Jew*-dy, *Jew*-dy, *Jew*-dy. Of all the hand-to-hand training Fleming had done at Bletchley, he liked boxing the best. No sneakiness to it, just square off and pound away.

"You surprise me old boy," he said finally.

"I couldn't resist not bringing an umbrella."

"Quite. You could still get pneumonia. It's damp and chilly in here."

"Americans don't get sick, you know that. They need to stay healthy so they can save the world from evil."

"Again."

"Correct."

"I suppose we should stay for the show." *Follow through.*

"Of course."

"What's Miss Ondra's story?"

"Mrs. Schmeling?"

"Yes."

"They say she loves him."

"More's the pity."

"Don't you have your hands full?"

Fleming did not respond. *Billie.*

"She's a beauty."

"I don't disagree."

"A gentleman wouldn't."

"No." *Meaning what, precisely?*

"She seems thick with that square-jawed young SS fellow. Stout as an oak."

Fleming did not answer. *The green-eyed monster eats at Mr. Hayseed. And me too.*

"I saw them getting into one of those Nazi Daimlers this morning."

Again Fleming did not reply. He pretended he was scribbling on his pad. *Not interested.*

"Fleming," Dowling said, "he's SS for Christsake."

The Englishman looked up at Dowling, keeping his face composed. "I'm aware of that," said.

The American paused a second, staring at his fellow reporter-cum-spy. "Of course," he said.

"She's not a Nazi, Dowling."

"Of course not."

"There are things I can't tell you."

"Of course."

"I have a favor to ask."

"Go ahead, no harm in asking."

"I need to get someone out of Germany, an engineer working on a secret anti-mine material. He wants to defect."

"A Nazi?"

"No, a Jew."

"I will leave a message with Hans. 'Any messages from the handsome American from Chicago?'"

"Fond of that 'handsome American' bit, are we?"

"The agent I replaced had his dick cut off by the Gestapo before they killed him. I may as well have some fun while I'm alive."

"How many have there been?" Fleming asked.

"Reporter types you mean?"

"Yes."

"I'm the third so far. And you, which number are you?"

"They don't tell us such things, but I'm led to believe I'm the seventh."

"Lucky number."

"If you say so."

"Not me. Look it up, you'll be amazed."

* * *

After the uneventful spar, Fleming and Dowling left together. The rain had stopped and the sun was breaking through rapidly thinning clouds. "I'll walk for a while," Fleming said curtly, heading east on Bismarkstrasse back toward the Adlon. *Bloody Americans,* he thought. *Getting into a Nazi Daimler indeed. Bloody women.* Lost in these thoughts, he did not notice the hulking black Daimler gliding along next to him at the curb, looking up only when two men, one tall and thin, the other short and stocky, both in overcoats and fedoras, blocked his path.

"Herr Fleming," the stocky one said.

"The very same," Fleming answered.

"You will come with us, please."

17.
Berlin
October 7, 1938, 1:00 p.m.

"You have some interesting things in your pockets, Herr Fleming."

"In England we don't do searches without good cause."

"That is why you are in decay."

Fleming remained silent.

"A list, for example, of various German government agencies, addresses, and telephone numbers."

"I'm a reporter. I often need to get quotes."

"Department of Raw Materials, Office for Racial and Settlement Questions, Waffen Supply Office, many others."

"My God, do you think I'm a spy?" *Shock*, Fleming said to himself, *that's the ticket.*

"Perhaps."

"I'd be the worst spy in history, then, carrying around a list of my contacts. You're joking of course."

"We don't joke here."

Here? Where is here? The Englishman knew where he was, the combined SS and Gestapo Headquarters on Prinz-Albrecht-Strasse. They had taken him in through a side entrance, but he had recognized the forbidding building, a former palace, then art school, then hotel—a short walk from his beloved Adlon—from the many times he had reconnoitered it on his visits to Berlin. It housed the Office of Surveillance and Prosecution in National Socialist Germany, the heart of the SS, as well as the notorious *Hausgefangnis*, what the Gestapo endearingly called its House Prison. He was pretty sure that's where he was, in a basement holding room, a cliché, really, with its cement floor, metal desk, and two metal chairs. His interlocutor, a man of about Fleming's age, thirty or so, was also a cliché: sallow skin, moist lips, a steady, undifferentiated look of contempt in his pale eyes. He wore the black uniform of the Gestapo, a lieutenant, small potatoes, but very dangerous for all that.

"You should, I daresay," Fleming responded, smiling. "Life is short and brutish otherwise."

"I will ask you again, where is your Professor Tolkien?"

"Do you think my answer will change from the one I gave you two minutes ago?"

"We have ways of getting the truth out of prisoners."

"Am I a prisoner?"

Before the lieutenant could answer, the phone on his desk rang. He picked it up, "*Ja, sind Sie bereit? . . . Gut.*" He returned the phone to its cradle, looked at Fleming, and, a gleam of delight appearing in his eyes, said, "Soon, Herr Fleming, your comedic act will cease."

* * *

Ten minutes later Fleming found himself naked, strapped to a chair with, oddly enough, its seat missing. While being strapped in by two nasty guards, he had noticed what looked like a tennis racquet on the floor beneath the chair. He had indeed lost his sense of humor. Nothing at Bletchley House had quite prepared him for this. Was he going to be buggered in some strange Germanic way? The desk across from him was empty except for a telephone and a small black metal box with a wire coming out of it and going down to the floor and heading ominously toward him.

The room was chilly, the cement floor damp and hard beneath his bare feet, his wrists and ankles already sore from the tight leather straps binding him to the chair. Worse than all this, his arse and balls and cock felt uniquely, uncomfortably, exposed as they hung down in close proximity to the thing he was beginning to realize was surely not a tennis racquet. Though the room was cold, he was sweating.

He was relieved for a second when the door swung open, but then he saw the look on the Gestapo lieutenant's face, a look of pure anticipatory delight, of ecstasy. The lieutenant withdrew an eight-by-ten photograph from a brown folder and held it in front of Fleming. He couldn't decipher it at first. Was it a skinned rabbit? Then he knew what the tennis racquet was. The photograph was of a man's mangled, bloody genitals. So much raw meat, swollen, but not quite beyond all recognition.

"I have several more here," the lieutenant said. "Would you like to see his face? He died shortly after."

Fleming stared in the lieutenant's eyes and saw in them nothing but pure sadism. He had found his calling, and not only was it legal, but it was highly prized by his superiors. Fleming did not answer.

"If you do not tell me where Professor Tolkien is, then I will push the red button on that little box," the lieutenant said, pointing at the box. "The wire mesh paddle beneath your chair will rise swiftly and with great force. After a few incorrect answers you will no longer be a man, and perhaps will be dead. I will take pictures and add them to my collection. On the other hand . . ."

The phone rang at this instant. Frowning, the lieutenant picked it up and placed it to his ear.

"*Nien,*" he said after listening for a second or two, and then, "*Ja.*"

* * *

They let him out at the same side entrance, an alley off of Wilhelmstrasse, that they brought him in through. Waiting for him on the cobblestones, his hands in his overcoat pockets, his collar turned up, was Kurt Bauer.

"Bauer," Fleming said.

"You are lucky, Herr Fleming."

"Lucky you say?"

"I heard by chance you were in the building."

"In the building? I was about to get my balls strafed off."

Bauer paused before answering. *He's waiting for a* danke, *the prick,* Fleming thought. *He's not what he says he is, I can tell by those heavy eyelids, always a giveaway.*

"Billie is waiting," said the young German.

"Where?"

"There." Bauer nodded toward Wilhelmstrasse, where another sleek black Daimler stood running at the curb, its windows darkened.

"Let's go."

"Did you get your belongings?"

"Yes."

"All there?"

Fleming's coat wallet, an aged leather affair from Smythsons of Bond Street, given to him by his brother Peter when he entered Sandhurst in 1927, was back in its usual place. The list of German government agencies was missing, as was the cash, a few hundred reichsmarks, and a hundred pounds or so.

"They took my cash."

Bauer shook his head and pursed his lips slightly, but said nothing. Fleming fingered his wallet through his cashmere coat at his breast. He had not had a chance to look into its hidden, silk-lined compartment, where he kept a medallion that was very dear to him, perhaps the only sentimental gesture he had ever allowed himself. He hoped it was still there. It would do the Germans no good at all.

At the top of the alley he could now see that Billie had emerged from the car and was waving him to her.

"Are you coming?" Fleming said to Bauer.

"No. Go. The car will return you to your hotel."

18.
Berlin
October 7, 1938, 3:00 p.m.

"Can I see the note?"

"Of course." Billie handed the sheet of plain white notepaper to Fleming. Embossed at the top was Franz Shroeder's name and title at Heidelberg University. Fleming read the note and passed it back to Billie. They were in the Professor's study in his apartment on Hermann Goering Strasse.

"He's taken the parchment," Billie said, "and the amulet is missing."

"The amulet?"

"Yes. He kept it in a secret compartment in his desk. It's gone."

"What amulet?"

"The beast."

"I see. The beast. He does not mention Tolkien."

"They must be together."

"Billie," Fleming said. "My dear girl. You are distraught. They're probably out for a jaunt. Tolkien has three days left on his visa. He mentioned he wanted to see the Black Forest."

"My father has never done anything like this. Since I can remember he has either been at university, in his study, or with me. He does not take jaunts, as you call them."

Fleming remained silent. Tolkien had never mentioned the Black Forest. He had a good idea of where he was really headed. He remembered now the angelic look in the don's eyes when they parted company last night. He was planning to flee. Bloody hell.

"What is this amulet you speak of?" Fleming asked.

"It's a stone carving with ruby eyes."

"What does it mean?"

"It's what my father is really working on for Himmler. A ritual that, when done in the right way in the right place with the right artifacts, is supposed the raise the dead."

"Raise the dead you say?"

"Yes."

"For Himmler?"

"Yes. Himmler wants to present Hitler with an unconquerable army."

"And the parchment, what is that?"

"The parchment has an incantation written on it. It and the amulet are the artifacts."

"How do you know this?"

"My father told me of course. You can't write about any of this, Ian. We'd all be killed. It is Himmler's project, you understand."

"I do, but tell me, it can't be true, can it? That the dead can be raised by this ritual?"

"I believe so."

"You believe so?"

"Yes."

Ian Fleming's interest in the paranormal extended perhaps to unusual sexual positions, nothing more, but now, seeing the grim set of Billie's beautiful face, a chill ran down his spine. She was serious, as serious as death.

"You seem so certain," he said.

"I am. There is a witness that is spoken of."

"A witness?"

"My father's schoolmate. He was with him when it first happened. They were twelve. Just boys. He spoke of it before he died recently."

"Is that how Himmler came to know?"

"I believe so."

"What do you mean by 'spoken of'?"

"Kurt told me there is a report on file."

"Ah, Kurt. Any details?"

"No. Just that. You won't write about this, will you?"

"Of course not. I do need to understand what's going on, though. I want to help you find your father, if indeed he's off on some adventure with the faeries. And I feel responsible for Professor Tolkien. If he overstays his visit, if he's off on some murky escapade inside Germany, there will be hell to pay."

"You were with Professor Tolkien last night. Did he mention any of this?"

"No," Fleming lied. "He told me he'd turned down Loening's offer to publish his book, that he was looking forward to returning to England, he missed his wife and children."

"My father doesn't even drive a car," said Billie. "I'm baffled."

"I doubt Tolkien does, either. Does your father have friends? Other professors, perhaps?"

"No, only Trygg."

"Where is Trygg, by the way?"

"I don't know."

"Does he drive?"

"Yes, he does."

"Does he own a car?"

"No. Not that I know of."

"Can he reach the steering wheel?"

"He sits on cushions."

"I see, it shouldn't be hard to find two absent-minded professors in tweed suits and a dwarf who looks like an ape but dresses like a toff scurrying about Germany. When do you think your father wrote this note?"

"Sometime after he left you last night, I assume."

"Where did he keep the parchment?"

"On his desk."

"How did you know about the amulet's hiding place?"

"Hiding place?"

"The secret compartment in his desk."

They had been standing this entire time in front of Professor Shroeder's desk, facing each other, the one-paragraph hand-written note dangling from Billie Shroeder's hand. Now she let the note drop abruptly to the carpeted floor, then crumpled herself in one swift movement into one of the room's two easy chairs, putting her hands to her face, the finger-tips to her forehead, the palms covering her nose and eyes. "Ian," she said, her voice unsteady, "I have been spying. I saw him once, when I was bringing him his tea, stooping under the desk. I knew that Himmler's people had been pressing him to locate the amulet. One day last week, while he was napping, I searched and found the compartment behind the deep bottom drawer. I saw the amulet. I wanted to end all this, this nightmare. I knew that Himmler must be losing patience, that he would harm my father if he did not get results soon."

"But you left it there?"

"Yes."

"Did you tell your father you knew where it was?"

"No."

"What were you thinking?"

"I didn't know what to do. At first I thought I would take it and throw it in a sewer. Then I real-ized that Himmler would keep pressing my father, that the pressure would kill him. Or Himmler would. Then I thought if things got very bad I could get Kurt to help, make a bargain—if I gave Himmler the parchment and the amulet, he would leave my father alone. I was paralyzed. I did nothing. I should have thrown it away. Now my father will be hunted down and killed."

"No one knows he's missing yet, or do they?"

"My father was not answering his phone, nor Trygg. I was worried. You were not in your room this morning. I called Kurt. He picked me up and drove me here. He saw the note."

"Did you tell him about the amulet?"

"Yes, yes, I felt I had to. My father is in great danger. Kurt said he would try to find him, bring him back."

"Where did this ritual take place when your father was twelve?"

"In Deggendorf, in the forest near his boarding school."

"What forest?"

"The Bavarian Forest."

"Do you know precisely where? That's a big place from the sound of it."

"No. He never told me, just that it's near his gymnasium, Metten Abbey."

"Would he head there?"

"I think so. He's said lately that if he ever found the amulet, he would bring it back to Metten and destroy it."

"How far is it from here?"

"Several hundred kilometers."

"I'll go after them."

"Take me with you."

Fleming did not answer. He bent down, picked up the note, and read it again.

"He has to go away for a few days. He says that you are to place yourself under my protection, that you are to do as I say until you are safely out of Germany. *Exactly* as I say."

"Yes, but I am in no danger. I don't understand why he would think I would leave Germany. What does he mean? Why *you*? Have you been talking to him? Is something happening that you won't tell me?"

"Nothing of the sort. I only spoke to your father the night you introduced me at the hotel and the next day at the interview."

Now Fleming could see that Billie was crying softly into her hands, shaking her head slightly from side to side, her beautiful, long brown hair shimmering as it caught the light from the room's lamps. With her legs tucked under her, she looked diminished, as small and as vulnerable as a child. "Oh, Ian" she said, "take me with you. I couldn't bear to wait here with you and father gone."

"Do you trust Kurt?"

"Yes."

"He works for the SS. He will surely tell his superiors, who will tell Himmler. There will be a small army out hunting for Tolkien and your father."

"No, Kurt promised he would not involve the SS."

"Does he know about the ritual? What your father was working on?"

"Yes, I told him, but only because I knew he would try to protect us if things got bad."

"Hasn't it ever occurred to you that Kurt might be watching you and your father? For Himmler?"

"Oh, Ian . . ."

"Where is he now?"

"He told me he would drive directly to Deggendorf."

"So you told him you think your father is heading to Metten."

"Yes."

"To destroy the amulet."

"Yes. I felt I had to."

"Did Bauer go by himself?"

"Yes."

Billie was sobbing now, the tears streaming under her hands and down her face. Fleming pulled his handkerchief from his breast pocket, knelt before her, gently tugged her hands away from her face, and began wiping her tears. She put her arms around his neck and pulled him to her. She put her face in his neck and her sobbing slowly subsided. He pressed against her and kissed her cheeks, tasting her tears, and said, "I will find them."

"Please Ian, please," she said. "Please be careful. Last night cannot have been our last. Please."

It did not surprise Fleming that he was aroused sexually. He liked tough women. When they submitted it was awfully erotic. But vulnerable was damn good too. Tears were an aphrodisiac. And pretty much everything else in between was alright as well. But now there was work to do, and, suddenly remembering something, he pulled back and took Billie by the shoulders. "I have some good news," he said. "A contact for your extraction."

Billie, tears still streaming down her face, shook her head. "I don't . . ."

"Your Jewish engineer in Magdaberg."

"Oh . . ."

Fleming reached for the small, leather-covered notepad in his jacket pocket. Taking a pen from the same pocket he scribbled on the pad, tore off the top sheet, and handed it to Billie. "It's a textile importer in Bremen. Ask for Herr Rhau. You are interested in buying a quantity of Suzhou silk. He will ask what quantity. You say you must first see the product. Understood?"

"Yes, thank you. This is priceless. Thank you . . . Ian . . . I must come with you to Deggendorf."

"Yes, you will. Your father wants me to protect you. I can't do that unless you're with me."

"Thank you."

"We'll go back to the hotel. I have to collect a few things. I'm sure you do too. We'll let it out we're heading on a short lover's jaunt. We *are*, in fact. Why not?"

19.

The Schorfheide Forest, North of Berlin
October 7, 1938, 6:00 p.m.

"Where are we, Trygg?" Professor Shroeder asked.

"We have just passed Eberswalde," the dwarf answered.

"How far have we come?"

"Fifty kilometers."

"Where will we cross?"

"The river is just ahead, a few kilometers."

"What's that ahead?" said Professor Tolkien from his seat in back of the Opel. "Slow down, Korumak."

In the flare of the Opel's headlights they could see in the middle of the road ahead a man in an ankle-length coat extending his arm toward them, palm up. Trygg slowed down and stopped some twenty feet away, but they were close enough now to see that the man was a German soldier, an officer by the cut and quality of his shimmering black leather coat and peaked, gold-embossed dress cap. Off to the side, the rear end of a large, black touring car faced the sky, it's front end in a ditch.

"Halt!" the officer said, even though they had come to a full stop. He walked to the driver's side of the car, his hand inside his coat. Trygg rolled down his window.

"What happened?" said Trygg, when the officer reached him. "Can we help?"

"A deer," the officer said, "a large one."

"What can we do?"

"We need your car."

"But . . . of course, we will do whatever you wish."

"Raus!" the officer said. They could see now from the insignia on his cap, which included the ever-present silver eagle clutching a swastika, that he was a full colonel in the Luftwaffe. They exited the car and walked toward the colonel, a red-faced man of forty or so with the slitted eyes of a pig.

"*Oberst*," a voice said, and they stopped. A stocky man in a long grey coat with a wide fur collar that extended almost to his waist had approached them. Trygg immediately swung into action. "Generalfeldmarschall," he said, bowing deeply. "We are honored."

Korumak hoped that the two professors remembered the simple instructions he had given them when they started out this morning. If they were stopped, he was to do the talking. If directly questioned, they were to stick to one story. *We are sightseeing. Professor Tolkien is a guest of Dr. Goebbels.*

"So, what have we here?" said Hermann Goering.

"We will commandeer the car," the colonel said. He had not come to attention, but he was standing tall in the field marshal's presence.

"I am talking to him," Goering said, nodding down at Korumak. "Are you a dwarf?"

"Yes, Field Marshal, I am."

"And your parents, are they dwarfs?"

"Yes, Field Marshal."

"We have dwarf servants at Carinhall, a husband and wife. They perform for us sometimes. It's great fun to watch."

Korumak remained silent. Rumors had reached him of evil doings, unspeakable doings, at Carinhall, Goering's lavish hunting lodge, which he knew was in the nearby Brandenberg Forest. In his breast pocket the little man had a slingshot with a small but very heavy old stone in its leather cup. He could kill Goering with it right now if he wished. No one would even see him do it, that's how deft of hand he was. But history would not change much, if at all, with the aviation buffoon dead, and surely he and the two professors in his care would die.

"You are well dressed," Goering said, mistaking, it seemed to Korumak, his silence for fear or reverence. He was wearing a dark gray worsted suit and vest, with a studded club collar and a black silk tie. On his feet were tiny black patent leather shoes.

"It is my master's wish," Trygg said.

"And who is he?"

"At your service Field Marshal," said Professor Shroeder. "Franz Shroeder, Professor Emeritus, Norse Mythology, Heidelberg. And this is my English colleague, here for a short visit, Professor Tolkien."

"Ah," said Goering. "I read of you two in *Der Sturmer* this morning. The old Norse gods are your specialty, no?"

The two dons nodded. "Yes, Herr Field Marshal," said Shroeder.

"Does Dr. Goebbels know you are trekking about in the woods?"

"I don't know, Herr Field Marshal. The interviews and filming were completed yesterday," Shroeder replied. "Professor Tolkien has a five-day visa. He wanted to see our beautiful forest country . . ."

"Stop, Herr Professor, I am not interrogating you." The general's tone had been sharp and his face glowering as he spoke to the white haired don, but now he broke out into a smile, a charming smile. "You are a loyal German. And you can do me a personal favor."

"Of course, Field Marshal."

"Take us in your car to Carinhall. You and Professor Tolkien and your servant can spend the night. It's the least I can do."

"Certainly, Field Marshal. We would be honored."

"I have guests tonight," Goering said. "There will be entertainment. You will mingle among the new

Norse gods." Turning to Korumak, Goering said, "Do you perhaps perform, Herr . . . ?"

"Korumak, Field Marshal. No, I'm afraid I have no talent along those lines."

"Korumak? Are you a Finn, perhaps?"

"No, German. From near Nebelhorn in the Bavarian Alps."

"It must be charming."

"It's a humble place, Field Marshal.

"And what brings you here, this close to the Polish border?" Though Goering's voice was friendly, even fatherly, his eyes were piercing, *as if,* Trygg thought, he knew that something was afoot and that I was the leader.

"We were trying for Eberswalde, Field Marshal," the small man answered, "but seemed to have missed it somehow."

"What is in Eberswalde?"

"A small museum the professors are hoping to visit."

"Ah, I will take you there myself tomorrow. I love museums, of whatever size."

20.
Wewelsburg Castle
October 7, 1938, 6:00 p.m.

"Where were your men, Lieutenant?"

"They were in position, Reichsfuhrer. One in front, one rear, one manning the listening equipment."

"Yet they neither saw nor heard any evil, so to speak, like the monkeys."

Silence.

"Correction, you say your man in front actually saw Tolkien go in around 7:00 a.m."

"Yes."

"Quite a knack for surveillance, that one."

Silence.

"But never saw him, or *any* of them, come out."

"Yes, Reichsfuhrer."

"They certainly *spoke* no evil. How could they, having nothing to report?"

"No sir."

"When did they discover they were gone?"

"At 10:00 a.m., Reichsfuhrer. The audio technician realized his lines were jammed."

"And his name is?"

"Sergeant Schneider, Reichsfuhrer."

"Where is he now."

"At Prinz-Albrecht-Strasse."

"*Gut*, we will deal with him later."

"Yes, Reichsfuhrer."

"And your search? You seemed truly optimistic. What happened?"

"Shroeder must have removed the amulet, Reichsfuhrer."

"And taken it with him?"

"Yes, Reichsfuhrer."

"To what end, do you think?"

Silence.

"To sell it to the highest bidder, perhaps? To give it to Neville Chamberlain? To Stalin? Perhaps he is an anglophile, our professor, or a communist."

Silence.

"Lieutenant, how would you like to be addressed as captain, or even major?"

"Of course I *would*, Herr Reichsfuhrer."

"Then give me some good news."

"We have every road south from Berlin to Deggendorf under surveillance. All train routes as well. They have not been seen."

"How are they traveling?"

"We assume by car, but we have also put men at several small airports in the vicinity of Deggendorf."

"The border crossings?"

"Yes, all alerted, Herr Reichsfuhrer."

"And the abbey?"

"I am heading there myself, now."

"You know that Heydrich has had trouble with them recently?"

"Yes, Reichsfuhrer."

"Two of their monks are our guests at Prinz-Albrecht-Strasse. They will not welcome you."

"No."

"You may tell the abbot, for me, that his priests will be released if he cooperates."

"But . . ."

"I will speak to Heydrich."

"Yes, Herr Reichsfuhrer."

"He will cooperate, of course."

"Of course, Herr Reichsfuhrer."

"It should not be hard to spot a dwarf, do you agree?"

"Yes, I do, Reichsfuhrer."

"I want him kept alive and brought to me, here at the castle."

"Yes, Herr Reichsfuhrer."

"Goering should not be the only one to have fun with dwarfs."

"Yes, Herr Reichsfuhrer."

"You know he has them copulate on a table in his banquet hall with large crowds watching?"

"No, Herr Reichsfuhrer, I did not."

"People bring their cameras."

"Yes, Herr Reichsfuhrer."

"And by the way, Lieutenant, I do not want Goering or Goebbels involved in this in any way. Is that understood?"

"Yes, Herr Reichsfuhrer."

"Where is the daughter?"

"I don't know, Herr Reichsfuhrer."

"Place her under arrest as soon as you find them. She has had too much freedom."

"Yes, Herr Reichsfuhrer."

"If they escape us, Lieutenant . . . Well, you will not let that happen."

"No, Herr Reichsfuhrer."

"*Gut*, you have the direct number to reach me. Someone will be at the phone around the clock. I will be here for the weekend."

Heinrich Himmler hung up the phone and looked out of the large double windows of his bedroom suite at the top of his triangular-shaped castle in the woods near Paderborn in northwest Germany. His wire-rimmed, pince-nez glasses were pinching his nose, so he removed them and rubbed away the itch with thumb and forefinger. Below were twenty men of varying size and age in purple-and-white-striped prison dress, each with a breast patch indicating his verminous blood, purple V's for Jehovah's Witnesses, yellow stars for Jews, and so on. They were mustering to be marched back to their camp a mile away. They were all coated in white from head to foot, having worked all day on removing the original plaster from the tower's walls and replacing it with local stone.

On a pedestal behind him was a picture book of busts of young Aryan men, the chiseled blonds who would someday make up the Master Race. He had been thumbing through this book when his adjutant knocked and announced the call from Lieutenant Bauer. He had been thinking of Bauer while looking at the pictures of those handsome Aryans.

The thought of sacrificing young Bauer was disturbing, but not very. He had had other pleasures in mind concerning Bauer, but if he failed he would have to be killed, or perhaps placed with the scum in the nearby camp. Or perhaps he would succeed in locating the runaway Professor Shroeder and his friends. Either way, there was pleasure in store.

21.
Carinhall
October 7, 1938, 10:00 p.m.

"Are we fully prepared, Captain Drescher?"

"Yes, Generalfeldmarschall," the Luftwaffe captain replied. "The keepers are ready, and the Messrs. Heck assure us the cow is in heat."

"Is that correct, Heinz? Lutz?"

"Yes, Generalfeldmarschall," the Messrs. Heck said in unison.

The four men—Hermann Goering, his adjutant, a square-jawed ex-paratrooper, and the Heck brothers, Lutz and Heinz, the directors of the Berlin and Munich zoos, respectively—were seated in oversized leather chairs in Goering's loft study at Carinhall, the aviation marshal's lavishly appointed hunting lodge in the forest north of Berlin.

"And our surprise guests, are they in hand?"

"They are resting in their rooms, Herr Generalfeldmarschall."

"Good. We will let them watch the breeding, then place them under arrest."

"Yes, Generalfeldmarschall."

"We will then see what Himmler and Heydrich are up to."

"Yes, Generalfeldmarschall."

"Do you know, gentlemen," Goering said to the Heck brothers, "that the Fuhrer will soon announce me as his successor?"

"No, Generalfeldmarschall," they replied. The awed looks on their faces were quite genuine. Adolph Hitler had replaced Christ in 1938 Germany, and his coterie were not just apostles or saints, they were demigods. A full-blown ur-god had now appeared in their midst. "We . . ."

"Yes, I know, you are honored to be in my presence. I have given him Austria, you see, his native country, and soon, with your help, I will give him a wild forest where the aurochs is the dominant beast, just as we Germans will soon be the dominant beasts in Europe."

The three men facing Goering—who was sitting in the deepest, plushest chair, as if on a throne—nodded in unison.

"And the dwarfs, Herr Generalfeldmarschall?" Captain Drescher said. "Shall we prepare them?"

"No," Goering replied. "They will not have to perform tonight. Tonight is for science and the advancement of knowledge, not comedic entertainment."

"Yes, Generalfeldmarschall."

"Are your men still out hunting?"

"Yes, Generalfeldmarschall."

"These two were difficult to capture, I understand."

"They are clever creatures, Herr Generalfeldmarschall," Drescher replied. "We caught them by blowing up a mine entrance and trapping them at the other end, in nets. We subdued them while they were slashing at the nets, trying to break free. Which was the more savage, the man or the woman, I do not know. The knives they used were quite extraordinary."

"Do you think you've found their habitat?"

"If so, it's a wild place, I'd say untouched since the Ice Age."

"And when was that?"

"Perhaps two million years ago, Herr Generalfeldmarschall."

"Are you serious?"

"Yes, Generalfeldmarschall."

"And our two, are they able to copulate? That's the primary thing."

"Yes, we believe so."

"Extraordinary knives, you say?"

"Yes, Generalfeldmarschall. Extremely sharp, razor sharp, and made of a metal I have never seen. The edges do not degrade, no matter what we do. And there are flecks of some kind of ore in them that we cannot identify."

"Yet they seem so submissive."

"Yes, Generalfeldmarschall, they have adapted to their new lives. The male is training as a footman, as you know, and the female in the kitchen."

"The last pair was not so hard to catch."

"Circus freaks. But alas . . ."

"Yes, I know, the human cannonballs have all deserted our circuses."

"They must have heard somehow . . ."

"Heard what, captain? We treat our dwarfs well. Surely public copulation is not torture."

"No, Generalfeldmarschall."

"Perhaps they have all gone to ground in the Bialowieza Forest," Goering said, smiling broadly, liking his own joke, "fashioning Ice Age tools and living in mines. A stroke of luck for us, no? The easier to round them up."

"Yes, Generalfeldmarschall."

At this moment, there was a knocking on the room's oak door. "Yes," Goering bellowed.

"Drinks, milord," a man's voice, deep and husky, said.

"Ah," said the field marshal. "Our refreshments. Come in. Enter."

A dwarf, in the red garb with gold epaulettes and buttons more fitting of a king's servant, came in wheeling a glass and polished wood serving cart laden with liquor, champagne, and their accoutrements, including ice, silver tongs, and crystal glasses.

"Shall I pour, milord?" the dwarf asked.

"No, leave us."

"Yes, milord."

"One moment, Tor," Goering said.

"Yes, milord."

"Have you met your fellow dwarf?"

"No, milord."

"Do all dwarfs wear beards?"

"Certain clans do, milord."

"Why is that?"

"I don't know, milord."

"Your beard is different from our guest, Korumak's."

"Yes, milord."

"Different clans, I suppose."

"I don't know, milord."

"You may go."

22.
Metten
October 7, 1938, 11:00 p.m.

"Our son is at school here," Billie Shroeder said.

"The abbey is closed, madam," said the SS corporal. As he spoke he shined a flashlight into the car, casting its stabbing beam first on Billie's face, then Fleming's, then doing a slow three-sixty of the interior. When he got to Billie's legs, she lifted her skirt an inch above her knee and smiled.

"He has been ill," Billie said.

"No one can enter."

"Why all the fuss?" Fleming asked, leaning and ducking slightly so that he could see across Billie in the driver's seat. Behind the corporal, four other soldiers were standing and warming their hands over a fire blazing out of a two-hundred-liter drum. Each had an Erma EMP-35 submachine gun slung over his shoulder, the elegant weapon that he knew Waffen SS Special Forces had recently been equipped with. Behind them the eighth-century abbey's massive wrought iron gate was shut and padlocked. The spacious stone courtyard was nearly pitch black, its outline made barely visible by the yellow light from one window above the abbey's imposing dome-shaped front entrance.

He and Billie had made it to Deggendorf by 9:00 p.m. and checked into an inn on the outskirts of the small city. Driving to the abbey, they had seen two SS staff cars parked in front of the Hotel Gasthof, the tallest building in the tiny town of Metten. Anticipating trouble, they had concocted their simple story and switched seats so that Billie could drive.

"Your husband?" the corporal said.

Fleming smiled and nodded.

"Yes, he's American," Billie said.

"No one can enter."

"Of course. Sorry for the trouble. Can we come tomorrow?"

"No. Now you must leave. *Now*."

23.
Carinhall
October 7, 1938, 11:00 p.m.

"That's the American bison on the left," said Trygg Korumak, "the European on the right. The European is the female."

"What in the world . . . ?" said Franz Shroeder.

"How do you know about this species?" Professor Tolkien asked.

"I have friends in the Great Last Forest, Dwerrow Forest, they call it," Korumak replied. "Where there are still bison."

"And what do men call it, this forest?" Tolkien asked.

"Bialowieza."

What do men *call it?* Tolkien said to himself. *Where did* that *come from?*

There had been something from the very beginning about Korumak that had not just intrigued Tolkien, but haunted him somehow, as if they had met as children and forgotten each other, or perhaps known each other in distant past lives. In the long day they had just spent in each other's presence, a day that was about to come to an obscene end, there had been little chance to converse, and when there had been a moment, Korumak had been singularly unforthcoming, his silence as solid and dense as a mountain. Now he seemed friendlier, but the scene below in the middle of Carinhall's great central hall was irresistible. John Ronald's questions would have to wait.

Looking down from the highly polished railing of the loft walkway that gave access to the bedrooms on the north side of the lodge, they could see two large, shaggy bison, one on the east side and the other on the west side of the immense room, each held in check by two muscular handlers gripping the ends of thick chains attached to metal collars on the animals' necks. The American bison was snorting and pawing the hardwood floor, the European straining from side to side on her forged leash.

Below glowing chandeliers that hung from massive floating oaken beams, stood Goering's guests for the weekend, perhaps fifty of what were obviously among Germany's military and political crème de la crème. Champagne glasses in hand, they were gathered around a space that had been cleared of furniture in the center of the room. Korumak seemed to know who many of them were. "That's Speer and his wife," he said quietly, nodding toward a dim corner where a tall, thin, balding man in a tuxedo was standing next to a woman in a red satin gown. Both were sipping champagne. "Hitler's best friend. And Bormann, another pig." Now the dwarf nodded toward the room's center, where a group of smartly dressed civilians and officers in beribboned uniforms were gathering along the velvet ropes and gold stanchions that marked off the makeshift arena.

Across the vast room—it was perhaps a hundred feet in length—they now saw Goering and his aide, a Luftwaffe captain, emerge from an inner room and approach the loft railing. The crowd acknowledged Hitler's aviation chief with a roar, many raising their glasses to him as he waved down at them, blessing them like the devil's vicar on earth.

Wagner could be heard from speakers concealed somewhere in the vast room, but only barely, as the cheering of the crowd was the dominant sound. That and the snorting and stamping of the bison as they strained toward each other on their leashes, the four handlers pulling hard along the flanks of the huffing creatures to hold them back. Goering raised his right hand high above his head, held it there for a long second or two, then swiftly brought it down, at which moment the handlers released the beasts.

"It can't be?" said Professor Shroeder, but indeed it was. The bison circled each other once and then suddenly were mating in the center of ring, while the crowd cheered. Bormann tossed his champagne glass at the male's head as he rutted, and many others followed suit.

Professor Tolkien looked on in horror at the scene below, at Bormann and his wife seizing full glasses of champagne from a passing servant, a dwarf with a beard like Korumak's, and throwing them at the cow this time. And across the room to Goering, who was smiling like a hyena and raising both of his arms in the air to acknowledge the adoring crowd below. The quiet, unassuming professor from Oxford knew in his bones that he was witnessing human beings at their very worst. Over the long remaining years of his life he would often ask God to forgive him for not turning away. He couldn't. He had to see and absorb and imprint on his brain the many faces of evil in that room.

24.
The Bergspitze Inn, Deggendorf
October 7, 1938, 11:00 p.m.

"So, do you still trust Kurt?" Fleming asked Billie.

"Yes, I do."

"If only *he* knew that your father and Tolkien had fled, then how did those troops come to be at the abbey?"

"Someone else must have . . ."

"Who?"

"I don't know. Honestly. But it can't have been Kurt. I'm certain. Ian, do you think father is in the abbey? Has he been captured do you think?"

"I told you, I don't think they'd go near the abbey. They may be college professors, but surely they must have realized that that would be the first place Himmler's hounds would be sniffing around."

"Perhaps they don't know that they are being looked for."

"I think they do."

"Why?"

"Tolkien told me that your father was given an ultimatum. Perform the ritual on Monday or else."

"Or else what?"

"You die."

"*I* die?"

"Yes, you. Do you think Himmler would be squeamish about threatening to kill you? Or actually killing you if it came to it? That was how they managed to persuade your father in the first place. They are thugs, murderous thugs."

Billie did not respond.

After seeing the troops at Metten Abbey's gate, the ride back to their small inn on a hill on the outskirts of Deggendorf had been a silent one. The English gentleman in Fleming had kept him from denouncing Billie as a fool for ever trusting her so-called college friend. Now he was doubly glad he had kept his counsel. The shocked look on her beautiful face reminded him of just how much a child she was, a child thrown against her will into a pit of vipers, one of whom she felt surely was her friend. Perhaps her eyes were now opening.

"My dear Billie," Fleming said, finally, "I envy your naïveté. I respect it, actually. There is a purity to it, a goodness that is rare in this world. But the Nazis have taken Austria, the Sudetenland, and made them into police states just as they have of Germany. Do you think Goering, Himmler, Goebbels and their ilk are patriots? No, far from it. They are indulging in personal fetishes and amassing fortunes, while gleefully enacting Hitler's insane policies."

"And Kurt?" Billie said. "You believe he is one of them?"

"Yes."

"It can't be . . ."

"He's a Nazi through and through."

"Ian . . ."

"I'm sorry."

More silence, while Billie composed herself, pulled her face into a sort of mask of acceptance. Fleming's heart melted at this effort of hers.

"I'll light a fire," Billie said at length, her voice low, close to a whisper. "It's cold up here."

"Good idea," Ian said. "While you're doing that I have something to attend to."

Fleming had assumed that Himmler's SS would be out in force looking for the Shroeder party, that

Kurt Bauer was a liar and had played Billie for a fool. He had therefore insisted, despite Billie's plea for speed, that they travel south via back roads. It would not do for the Nazis to intercept a car containing Franz Shroeder's daughter and an English reporter heading toward Deggendorf. It had taken them almost eight hours as opposed to the five or six the trip south normally took, but he had been right. If troops were at the abbey, they were also covering the main roads and railroad stations along the way.

Putting these thoughts aside, the Englishman reached for the small canvas duffle bag he had lugged with him from Berlin and pulled out the two-way backpack radio that Bletchley had had made for him specially and that Hans the bartender had delivered to his room at the Adlon just before he and Billie had headed south. He could hear Billie's movements behind him and the crackling of the kindling that their ruddy-faced innkeeper had left in the room's large stone fireplace for them. The attic room, which Ian had specifically asked for, *was* cold, but soon it would be warm, at least in the vicinity of the fireplace.

He lifted the heavy radio by its side handles and set it down in the middle of the small room. Then he pulled up the antenna and set the frequency selector to random. Hans had said that the dry cell battery, which made the bloody thing so heavy, was fresh, but had packed him an extra one anyway. They last only thirty minutes or so at the most, his lab trainer at Bletchley had told him, so make the most of your time. When the neon indicator turns red, change the battery. Otherwise, just push the on switch, and speak your caller ID into the handset.

"What are you doing?" Billie asked.

Fleming had lifted the handset, but not turned the radio on. The moment has come, he said to himself.

"Frequency hopping," he said.

"Frequency hopping?" Billie was eyeing the radio like it was something that had landed in the room from outer space.

"Yes," Fleming said. "Do you know Hedy Lamarr?"

Silence. Then, "Do *you*?"

"I do, in fact. I met her in Paris in the spring. She was going through a divorce at the time."

"Ian . . . What is that machine?"

"It's a two-way radio. Half-duplex, point-to-point."

"What in the world . . . ?"

"It's a long story, Billie. I'm going to get us help."

"But won't the Nazis be listening? I understand they monitor all of the frequencies all of the time."

"That's where Hedy comes in. She and her first husband—she was divorcing her second in Paris—invented this frequency hopping thing. It's based on a player piano."

"A player piano?"

"Don't ask me why or how."

Silence, then: "You really *are* a spy."

"I'm afraid so."

"Is that why you went out earlier?"

"Yes."

"Where did you go?"

"To scout out a meeting place."

"Who are we meeting?"

"Not *we*, me."

"Who?"

"Someone to help me find your father and Tolkien."

"Is that who you're contacting on that machine?"

"Yes, the Americans. They're on the ground here."

"How can they help?"

"You saw those troops ringing the abbey. We may have to storm the place."

"Ian."

"Yes?"

Billie had taken a step toward Fleming. She had removed the down quilt from the room's four-poster bed and placed it on the floor in front of the fire, the pillows as well.

"Shall I get undressed? Are we . . . ?"

"Yes and yes," Fleming replied. "Get under that quilt. I'll join you in a sec."

Billie smiled, reached around, and unhooked the back of her calf-length wool skirt. It dropped to the floor at her feet, revealing her long, shapely legs in garter belt, nylon stockings and black panties. Fleming devoured this sight.

"Go ahead," he said, turning back to the radio and pushing the on button. "I'll join you in a sec."

25.
Carinhall
October 7, 1938, 11:00 p.m.

Suddenly the room below was filled with smoke, huge white clouds of it quickly filling its four corners and billowing up to the loft railing. Tolkien caught a quick glimpse of Goering being pulled into a room by his aide, then felt himself being tugged violently from behind. "Put this on your face," Trygg Korumak said, handing him a towel soaked in water. Another dwarf, a woman with braided auburn hair and deep-set green eyes, was pulling at Franz Shroeder and handing him a damp towel as well. "Follow us," Korumak said, when the professors had their faces covered.

They did, scurrying along the side of the open loft hallway until they reached a recessed door, which the woman unlocked with a long bronze key. They entered a room the size of a large closet. A storage room, it seemed to Tolkien, who bumped into a bucket from which protruded several mop handles. "What was that?" Tolkien said, as the woman locked the door behind them.

"Not now," Trygg replied.

The room was pitch black, but the woman had found a chain hanging from the ceiling and pulled down a set of collapsing stairs. "Up!" she said. "Go!"

"Drop the towels," Korumak said, "you won't need them now."

On their hands and knees in the dark attic, they followed the small woman and Trygg, who were walking, for about a hundred feet. When they halted, Tolkien, whose eyes had adjusted to the darkness, watched as the woman opened a small window and looked out quickly. Turning to face them, she motioned *come*. Tolkien now realized that Franz Shroeder, who had not said a word, was breathing heavily. "Franz, are you alright?" he said to the old man, who was now kneeling with his head down.

"I'm . . ." Shroeder said, but before he could finish his sentence, Korumak was tugging at Tolkien.

"You first," he said, pushing the Englishman firmly but gently to the open window. Looking out, Tolkien saw a rope ladder leading to a roof some twenty feet below. Standing on this roof, holding onto the nether end of the ladder, was the dwarf he had seen serving champagne to Goering's guests not five minutes ago.

"Go!" the woman said.

26.
Berlin
October 7, 1938, 11:30 p.m.

"There is a message for you," Hans said.

"From whom?"

"The caller ID was 007."

As he spoke, Hans was pouring Rex Dowling his favorite drink, Glenlivet with two ice cubes. Now he placed it on an *ADLON*-embossed cocktail napkin and slid it gently toward the American, who was smiling as if they were discussing the weather, which had turned cold, or women, whom they both liked at warmer temperatures. Smiling, his face a mask of idle pleasantness, the reporter picked up the drink. As he sipped, the slight narrowing of his blue eyes over the rim of his crystal rocks glass transmitted a concise message to the bartender. *Go on.*

Hans nodded and took a moment to scan the thickly carpeted, dimly lit room, its small, round, randomly placed tables and corner banquettes filled with people quietly talking and sipping drinks. Hans knew most of them, including the Gestapo agents in civilian dress who stopped by almost every night to glare at the overseas press contingent and intimidate any tourist or business traveler who might be thinking of undermining the Reich. No foreigner was really welcome in Berlin in 1938.

"How is your drink?" Hans asked. "To your liking?"

"*Ausgezeichnet*", Dowling replied, "*danke.*"

"Your German is terrible, Herr Dowling," said Hans, loud enough for the agents at the nearest table to hear, then, his voice lower, "007 needs firepower."

"What kind?"

"Small arms, rifles, machine guns."

"Men?"

"Yes."

"Have you spoken to your uncle?"

"Yes. He will extract from Czechoslovakia, but otherwise 007 is on his own."

"Leaving him high and dry?"

"Chamberlain just finished the Munich agreement. He wants no complications."

"So Meppen is cancelled."

"Yes."

"Did 007 ask for me?"

"Yes."

"Where do we rendezvous?"

"Rex, I didn't think you really cared . . ."

"*Hans.*"

"In the forest in Deggendorf."

"Do you have the coordinates?"

"Yes."

"Now?"

"Immediately, if not sooner."

"Can you help?"

"Yes, my brother as well."

"Weapons?"

"Yes, a few."

"Men?"

"No, just Jonas and me."

"Transportation?"

"Yes. I have a colleague who has a garage on Hermann Goering Strasse. He'll lend us a truck with no history."

"We have to leave now, tonight."

"I need an hour."

"You'll lose your job."

"It's time I joined the underground anyway."

"Can you reach 007 to confirm?"

"Yes."

"You can tell me about that scar on the ride to Deggendorf. Is there a special story, or was it just boring old shrapnel?"

"A story involving an American and a woman."

"Good, it will help us pass the time."

27.
The Schorfeide Forest
October 7, 1938, 11:30 p.m.

"What happened back there?" Professor Tolkien asked.

"Sleeping gas," Korumak replied.

"Sleeping gas? That smoke?"

"Yes. It doesn't last long. Five minutes at the most."

"Who . . . ?"

"The dwarf servants."

"What is sleeping gas?"

Korumak did not answer. He stared at Tolkien. "Your face is bleeding," he said. "I'll get you some water in a moment."

"Why?" Tolkien asked. He put his fingers to his throbbing head, where he had bumped it against something very hard, and then along his cheek, which stung and was indeed bleeding.

"Goering was going to question us," the dwarf replied, "then lock us up and notify Himmler. They overheard him."

"Where are we?"

"In a mine," replied Trygg Korumak. "Not far from Carinhall."

"Why did you blindfold us?"

Once clear of Carinhall, the small group had gathered in the forest at the foot of a wooded hill to get their bearings. There, Korumak, in a husky whisper, had simply said, "Follow me. Do not speak." Twenty minutes later, after clawing their way through a ten-foot-high high wall of dense brush, they had emerged in a small, moonlit valley on the opposite side of the same hill. Up and over and around what seemed like a dozen boulders, they went, until finally Trygg halted and handed Tolkien and Shroeder large cotton kerchiefs, saying sharply, *put these over your eyes.*

"The entrance is secret," the dwarf replied.

"I couldn't find it again in a million years."

"Perhaps. Then again, perhaps you could. We are all capable of much more than we realize."

"How long will we stay?"

"An hour, no more."

"Where are we going?"

"To meet with friends, water people."

"Water people?"

"Yes, they will guide us to the Oder and then take us downriver to a place where we can cross back into Germany."

"We're walking?"

"Part of the way, yes, tonight and all day tomorrow."

"And then where?"

"To Metten, to find the Devil's Canyon."

"The Devil's Canyon?"

"Men call it that."

"What men?"

Tolkien and Korumak were sitting cross-legged in front of a small fire in a circular cavern they had reached by a long series of steeply descending rough-hewn stone steps. At the beginning of the descent, Tolkien had struck his head on the ceiling of the tunnel. After that, he had crouched very low, gripping the back of Professor Shroeder's coat with a strength he did not know he had. Along the cave's perimeter were five stone platforms carved with precision out of the cave's wall. On each was a thick straw mat covered by a wool blanket. Against the wall near the stairway stood a half dozen axes, their curved, mace-like blades shimmering in the firelight. From an arched opening to their right, the voices of Professor Shroeder and the two dwarfs who had lead them out of Goering's hunting lodge and into the forest could be heard approaching. Tolkien heard the words *le-vasst-u-rukhas*, or rather sounds to that effect. *Ancient Norse?* he said to himself, and then, *no not at all like it. Then what?* Before he could ponder more, Korumak replied, "The men who discovered it."

"You mean Professor's Shroeder's canyon, the ritual . . ."

"Yes."

Tolkien remained silent. He had studied the dwarfs of Scandinavian legend extensively. They were, above all else, secretive. They had a language of their own, which they never spoke in the presence of men or other races, not even the gods, and which they rarely committed to paper or writing of any kind. Their dwarf names did not even appear on their gravestones. Great miners and metal workers, they were also fierce warriors, with the strength and endurance of three or four strong men. They were cunning and loved gold, and because he had portrayed them this way in *The Hobbit*, the managing partner at the publishing house he had visited yesterday had told him, smiling broadly, that he was seen to be simpatico with the Reich regarding the Jewish problem. *The Jewish Problem. Bloody Nazis.* Thank God he had refused to sign that vile "I am not a Jew" oath. He would write a proper letter of rebuke when he returned home. If he returned home.

"Are the two servants your countrymen?"

"Yes."

"I am in their debt."

"We all are."

Before he could speak again, Shroeder and the Carinhall dwarfs entered the round cave laden with woven baskets and stone jugs filled with water.

Tolkien looked upon them, particularly Shroeder, with something akin to shock. The German professor was dressed in brown woolen leggings and fur-covered boots that laced to just below his knees. On top he wore a tunic of the same dark color and material, and over this a hooded, dark green woolen cape that reached nearly to his feet. Leaning on his cane, the old German professor looked tired and pale, and sad somehow, as if he had just come to terms with an unhappy fate. His face bore the signs of scratches and bruises that had been cleansed but were still raw. Yet there was a presence to him, a light in his eyes that Tolkien had not seen before and indeed never expected to see in the mild-mannered old professor. Was he talking to the Carinhall dwarfs in their language?

The dwarfs had changed clothes as well, their servants' livery exchanged for sleeveless leather tunics with silver buckles over woolen blouses and leggings. The metal hobs on their leather boots scraped on the stone floor. The woman handed baskets filled with similar clothing to Tolkien and Korumak.

"These are Dagna and Gylfi," Korumak said. "Professor Tolkien."

The dwarfs bowed deeply, but said nothing.

"Thank you," Tolkien said. "For saving us, and for these," indicating the baskets of what looked like warm and comfortable clothes. He noticed now that Dagna and Gylfi were the same fair coloring as Korumak, with the same thick auburn hair, the same hooked noses and deep-set piercing green eyes. Gylfi had braided his beard in two places, like Korumak wore his. If she had worn a beard, the Englishman would have taken Dagna, the woman, for a man.

"We'll change in there," Korumak said, nodding toward the anteroom, "and tend to your bruises."

Before turning to leave, Tolkien noticed that the basket that Gylfi was carrying held what surely looked like loaves of bread, dark and round, and steaming hot. *How in the world?* he said to himself. But that, and other questions, many other questions, could wait. He was dirty, and bruised, and thirsty, and hungry, and drained of energy. Yet he had no doubt that all of that would very soon be remedied, that, though only three days ago he was lecturing at Oxford, this cave, and the path he was about to embark upon were where he should be, where God in his wisdom wanted him to be.

28.

Carinhall
October 8, 1938, 2:00 a.m.

"How was the flight, sergeant?" Hermann Goering said.

"Fine, Generalfeldmarschall."

"Surprised to get such orders?"

"No, Generalfeldmarschall. We are always ready."

"They have a two hour head start."

"That will not be a problem, Generalfeldmarschall."

"Do you know what you're tracking?"

"I was told two men and three dwarfs—two male dwarfs and one female."

"Correct. They may have gone in different directions."

"I brought five hounds, Generalfeldmarschall, and five Schäferhunde."

"Fighting animals?"

"Yes. The hounds are for tracking only."

"You know I keep mountain lions here?" said Hermann Goering.

"Yes, Generalfeldmarschall."

"Four altogether, all full grown. Two males and two females."

"Yes, Generalfeldmarschall."

"You say your hounds are top quality, pedigreed?"

"Yes, Generalfeldmarschall."

"German hounds?"

"They are Flemish hounds, Herr Generalfeldmarschall."

"Yes, the half-breed Flemish. They will be under our flag as well, soon enough. What are your hounds' names?"

"Hildegarde, Trudy, Greta, Marlene and Marie."

"All female?"

"Yes, Generalfeldmarschall."

"You are an infantryman, I take it."

"Yes, Generalfeldmarschall, regular Heer."

"The Luftwaffe will win the war, not the Army, do you agree, sergeant?"

"Yes, Generalfeldmarschall."

"Still, you have your uses."

The sergeant, in a long, black, hooded leather coat, did not reply. He had not been asked a question. He and Goering were standing in Carinhall's Belgium block courtyard. The light from the cast iron lanterns on either side of the lodge's massive front door bathed their faces. On the grass that surrounded the lodge's forty-foot-high flagpole in the center of the expansive courtyard, the five bloodhounds sat on their haunches, their eyes fixed on their trainer and lord and master, Army Sergeant Klaus Klein. Behind them, standing at ease near the truck they arrived in, were four more Army regulars, all in the same long, black, hooded leather coats as Klein. Each had a submachine gun slung over his shoulder. They were all well over six feet tall. The insignia on the arm patches was the stylized face of a German Shepherd baring its fangs. In the truck's open bed the five German Shepherds were standing, looking over at Sergeant Klein.

"They seem quite ready," Goering said, looking over at the shepherds.

"They know there is work to do," Klein replied.

"Will they kill a man?"

"On my command, yes."

"You know I want these escapees brought here alive?"

"Yes, Generalfeldmarschall."

"I want no interference from any other service branches."

"Yes, Generalfeldmarschall."

"Am I quite clear?"

"Yes, Generalfeldmarschall."

"Good. Now tell me, what do you need?" Goering asked.

"Articles of clothing would be best, Generalfeldmarschall."

"Captain Drescher is in the kitchen, inside and down the hall to your right. We have plenty of clothing. They all left in a hurry."

The sergeant remained silent.

"My mountain lions have eaten dogs, Sergeant," said Goering. "They've developed a taste for them."

Silence.

"You see what I'm driving at, don't you? You are an intelligent man, a veteran non-commissioned officer of the German Wehrmacht."

"Yes, Generalfeldmarschall."

"Good. I know then that you will not fail."

29.
Metten Abbey
October 8, 1938, 6:00 a.m.

"This part of the abbey was consecrated in 766," Father Wilfrid, the abbot of Metten Abbey, said.

"I have been respectful, my good priest," Kurt Bauer replied, "but my patience is not limitless. You insist on believing that I am interested in the history of your abbey. I am not."

"There are no tunnels here," said the priest, "as I have said. But it appears you do not believe me."

Father Wilfrid, a man in his early sixties, sat at his desk in his very simple study-cum-office in Metten Abbey's central tower. These words he had just spoken, and the ones last night, were, combined, far more than all those he had uttered in the last ten years. On the day he was chosen as abbot in 1928, he said mass in the abbey's twelve-hundred-year-old chapel, gave communion to the community of monks and oblates who had selected him, then said a word of humble thanks to each of them. Since then his speech was limited to "good morning," "good afternoon," and "good evening," to those few monks he encountered in his daily routine. Across from him in an upright wooden chair sat SS Lieutenant Kurt Bauer, his young, ruddy face clean-shaven, his blond hair combed and severely parted, his blue eyes pitiless. Though a dedicated monastic, Father Wilfrid was not unaware of the events transpiring in his country. This, he said to himself, is the face of the new Germany.

"Do you know that the German government is holding two of your fellow monks on suspicion of treason?" Bauer asked. "They were captured distributing seditious material in Munich."

"Naturally word of these men has reached me." The abbot fingered the wooden crucifix he wore around his waist, thinking, as he did, of the manuscript under glass in the abbey's library, the one from which the ancient *Vedo Retro Satana* formula had been discovered in 1415, the same canto that was imprinted on the Saint Benedict medal he wore around his neck. *Step back Satan. Step back Lieutenant Bauer. Step back Adolph Hitler.*

"They may be hanged."

This was not the first time Father Wilfrid had heard the young Nazi use the word hanged. *Traitors are hanged*, he had said last night. *I have the authority to execute you on the spot if you do not cooperate.* This was only moments after his men had nearly broken down the abbey's six-hundred-year-old front door, the loud thud, thud, thud of rifle butts against solid oak having roused him just in time from the rope cot he slept on in a small room behind his ground floor office.

"In know of no tunnels in the abbey."

"You *know* of no tunnels in the abbey," Bauer said. "I see. Who is your oldest priest? The one here the longest."

"Father William. He is ninety-five."

"My grandfather was a student here."

"Yes, as you've said."

"He told me there were catacombs under the abbey and a tunnel leading into the forest, so that the monks could escape if necessary."

"Catacombs, yes, but no tunnel. You may look again if you wish. Your men were down there for hours."

Forty or so German soldiers had searched every room in the abbey overnight, as well as the catacombs, with no results that Father Wilfrid was aware of. Every one of the abbey's fifty monks was roused from his bed, his person searched, and his room ransacked. Three or four locations on the stone walls of the catacombs were pierced by soldiers wielding pick axes. How these areas were chosen, Father Wilfrid did not know. He only knew that after hours of attacking the wall only more stone was to be seen. He had tried to tell Bauer that the abbey's foundations were said to be thirty feet thick, but to no avail. Bauer's soldiers were now lounging, some obviously exhausted, in the large rotunda that served as an entry hall for the abbey. During the night, the sounds of trucks on the abbey grounds and the muffled clanging of soldiers setting up camp had occasionally reached the abbot's ears.

I am looking for three men. Rather, two men and a dwarf, Bauer had barked last night. *Do you have any guests?*

No, we do not.

I also understand there is a tunnel here, an escape tunnel. Where is it?

There is no such tunnel here.

Where is your office?

There.

These two men will guard you.

"When did Father William come to the abbey?" Bauer asked now.

"When he was seventeen, in 1872."

"My grandfather mentioned a novitiate named William who knew about the tunnel."

"That must be Father William."

"Where is he now? I would like to speak to him."

"Morning prayers will be starting soon. And then we have a simple breakfast. Can you wait? Father William is old and not well, and probably already in a shocked state from the search last night. His routine will settle him down."

Bauer did not answer immediately. Father Wilfrid, who was himself exhausted, leapt into the breach.

"Lieutenant, my dear sir, the abbey is occupied and surrounded. Father William is ninety-five and frail. We have neither weapons nor means of travel. We are German citizens. We want to help the Reich. Just give him an hour to recover from last night. Shall I have him here for you in my office at, say, seven?"

"Very well," Bauer said. "But not here. You will take me to his room at seven. And until then you will stay here under guard. You know too much already."

30.
The Schorfeide Forest
October 8, 1938, 6:00 a.m.

"How far are they, do you estimate?"

"A kilometer, two at the most."

Professor Tolkien, who had stayed at the rear of the single file of trekkers throughout the long night, had moved to the front to be near Trygg Korumak.

"We have to stop," Tolkien said. "We can't outrun them."

"I agree," said Korumak, who the next instant was standing on a five-foot-high boulder gesturing to the rest of the party, who had all stopped at the crest of a low ridge to listen to the frenetic howling and yelping of the pack of bloodhounds at their heels. *How did he move so quickly?* Tolkien asked himself, not for the first time since their journey began. *Did I actually see him leap onto that boulder?*

"Goering has sent out hounds," Korumak said to the group once they had gathered at the foot of the boulder. When he first heard the howling an hour ago, very much in the distance, Tolkien hoped it was a pack of wolves surrounding a wounded stag, and had said as much to Professor Shroeder. But the sounds had followed them until there was no other conclusion to be drawn. Wolves did not bark. Wolves did not hunt men.

"How far are they?" asked Professor Shroeder.

"A kilometer or two."

They had marched in single file all night, stopping once for fifteen minutes in a dry streambed to rest their legs and eat some of Dagna's bread. The terrain was gentle at first as they passed through Goering's hunting park, but had gotten rougher as, led by Korumak, they made their way due east. The last ten kilometers had been rocky, a glacial spill, Korumak had called it. Boulders large and small were interspersed among the tall pine and oak trees that covered the forest. The bread—it must have been the bread, Tolkien said to himself—had not only sustained them, but given them energy they could never have dreamed of having after eating normal food. Even Shroeder, seventy-eight years old, had not complained as they walked rapidly, staying within inches of each other, along deer paths, under dense foliage, and over bramble-covered ridges, through the black, moonless night. Over the last couple of kilometers the false dawn had dimly lit their way and now they could see a thin line of red at the horizon.

"How many, do you think?" Tolkien asked.

"A dozen hounds, a half-dozen men," Korumak replied.

"How much time?"

"Ten minutes for the dogs, twenty for the men."

"I have an idea," Tolkien said. He had been scanning their surroundings, picking features out of the murky light that spread like fog when night is on the precipice of day. Behind them was another rock formation, boulders piled on boulders. One group formed a triangular opening the size of a small man.

"Gylfi, Dagna, everyone, can I have your scarves?" said Tolkien.

"Yes," five voices replied at once, as all began unwrapping their thick, brown woolen scarves.

"Franz," Tolkien said. "Where is the amulet?"

"In a pouch around my neck."

* * *

Ten minutes later, the group was huddled behind the boulder that Korumak had been standing on. Dawn had not yet broken, but the red line at the horizon behind them had thickened. The men on their feet, the dwarfs on piles of rocks, they peered carefully over the boulder, eyeing the ridge, perhaps thirty yards away across the forest floor, the ridge they had climbed up and over and down to get to this spot. Suddenly the first dog, a huge black and brown hound appeared at the top of the ridge and began howling at the highest decibel she could reach, the sign to her handlers that she had cornered or treed her prey. Then the others appeared, and the shepherds and the hounds together began to viciously tear at the scarves that lay at the top of the ridge. Salivating and snarling they fought each other for the shredded pieces of wool.

"Now, Franz," Tolkien said.

Professor Shroeder reached inside his tunic, pulled out the amulet with his right hand, stood, and raised it above his head. The hounds stopped in unison and turned to look at it. The group could see the dogs' eyes glowing in the semi-darkness as they whimpered and stared up at the small black beast in the hand of the white-haired old man. After perhaps two seconds, the dogs, all howling a much different howl than had been heard before—these were howls of terror—turned and fled. As Professor Shroeder, his hand trembling, returned the amulet to its leather pouch, Tolkien saw it for a split second. Its ruby eyes were aglow. Shroeder slumped to the ground. Before anyone could tend to him, the sounds of heavy trampling and crashing through bramble could be heard and in the next instant five tall men, giants it seemed in their long black coats, the hoods up against the cold, were standing in a row at the crest of the ridge.

"Wait," Tolkien whispered, his hand up.

Turning, Tolkien watched the first sliver of the sun breach the horizon. He waited until its bright rays shone through the triangle behind them, directly into the faces of the five German soldiers opposite. They all shielded their eyes with their hands. This was the last human gesture they would ever make. Tolkien said, "Now," and Korumak, Gylfi, and Dagna leaped out from behind the boulder and with blinding speed hurled their axes at the men. Gylfi and Korumak each flung a second ax. All of this took no more than one second. Tolkien, watching over the boulder, never saw the axes fly, but the result was plain to see. Five tall, black-clad men, each with an ax buried in his chest.

31.

The Bavarian Forest, Near Deggendorf
October 8, 1938, 8:00 a.m.

From the second floor window of the abandoned mill, Ian Fleming had an unobstructed view of the old but still sturdy plank bridge that Dowling and whatever help he could muster would be crossing to reach him. Fleming had stumbled upon the bridge and the mill last night while looking for a decent rendezvous spot. He had been hoping for a sheltered rock shelf or an enclosed meadow, and was gleeful at his luck in finding the mill, which, by the looks of it, had not been in use for decades if not longer. He had arrived before dawn, and with the first light began training his small field binoculars on the bridge and the overgrown dirt road that led to it, listening all the while for out-of-place sounds in the thick surrounding forest. The small tributary of the nearby Danube that powered the mill flowed gently below his de-glazed window, unimpeded by a paddle wheel, which he surmised had been removed by the owner or more likely stolen years ago. Behind him on the stone grist cap he had laid out a topographical map of the area, with likely routes to Metten Abbey, which was some three kilometers away to the west. Following the un-named tributary seemed like the most direct route.

A movement on the opposite bank of the stream drew his eye. He raised the glasses and immediately saw three men on the far side of the bridge: Dowling and the Kaufmann brothers, Hans and Jonas. All three had submachine guns slung over their shoulders. Fleming pulled from his jacket pocket the white handkerchief that was the prearranged all-safe signal and hung it from a crevice in the crumbling brickwork just below the window. Looking again, he saw Dowling look up at him through his own field glasses, then put them away and cross the bridge with his companions.

32.
Metten Abbey
October 8, 1938, 8:00 a.m.

When he first dismissed the annoying and too-clever abbot and entered Father William's damp and bare monk's cell, Kurt Bauer wished he were not in his Gestapo uniform, which he felt would be frightening to the old priest, cause him to stammer or go mute. He had seen these reactions before, and in much younger men. He had brought along Waffen SS gray field fatigues, but there was no time to change. It turned out, however, that his black officer's regulars, as Heydrich and Himmler had styled them, had had the opposite effect. The wrinkled, wafer-thin, bald as a cue-ball old monk could not stop talking.

Yes, I remember the two boys, he had said, *Franz and Ernst. Your grandfather Ernst, how marvelous. They fed the kitchen dog, Bridget, that's how I met them. Tunnel from the abbey? No. Just catacombs. We were not allowed down there. Father Adelbert? Yes, of course. He was as silent as stone, always shirking his duties, always in the library. His eyes . . . his eyes were a startling gray. He never looked at you. A tunnel you say? No, not here, and I've been here seventy-seven years. I've been in the catacombs many times now. No, no tunnel there. But there was a tunnel in the forest. Young Franz said he saw Father Adelbert disappear into it one day. Disappear, he said, a strange choice . . .*"

"Stop," Bauer said.

"Stop? Of course. But there is no tunnel here, I'm sure . . ."

"Where was the tunnel in the woods?"

"I, I don't know?"

"Are you sure?"

"Yes, I am."

"Where did Franz tell you the tunnel entrance was?"

"He didn't tell me. I don't know."

"You don't know where it is, or he didn't tell you?" The priest was frightened now, but that was good. He was too addle-brained to formulate a proper lie, to even think of deception, but in case he did, well, it was not for nothing that Heydrich's black-uniformed elite had spread terror among the German people.

"He didn't tell me."

"Is it far?"

"I don't think so. The boys were not allowed to go into the forest."

"But Franz went."

"Yes."

"And young Ernst, my grandfather."

"Yes."

"Where did they go?"

"I don't know. What . . . ? Why do you want to know? They were good boys."

"Father William, you are a Catholic priest. You have been taught that the end never justifies the means, that morality is not relative."

"Yes, yes I have."

"So you know that if you are lying to me for some higher good, you will surely have a stain on your soul."

"Yes, I know."

"There is also an earthly punishment in store for you if you are lying to me. I see you have some teeth left."

"Yes, I do."

"I will break them off with a hammer and feed them to you. After that the torture will start. Do you understand?"

"Yes, yes, I do."

33.

The Bavarian Forest, Near Deggendorf
October 8, 1938, 9:00 a.m.

"That's a hell of a story," said Rex Dowling. "Raising the dead. It's a joke of course. You're running some kind of double reverse."

"Double reverse?" said Fleming

Ian Fleming, Rex Dowling, and the Kauffman brothers were sitting cross-legged in a circle on the mill platform with Fleming's map on the floor between them. Dusty rays of morning sunlight were slanting down on them through jagged gaps in the pitched roof where planking had once been. The Englishman had drawn a circle in red ink around the location of the abandoned mill and another around Metten Abbey, which was symbolized on the map with an armored angel slaying a dragon at his feet. One of the streams of sunlight fell directly on this symbol.

"It's a football term," Dowling said. "American football."

"I'm afraid not."

"You believe it's true?"

"Shroeder says he saw it work twice and did it himself years later."

"Like Lazarus?"

"No, animals. A lynx, a dog, and a cat."

"Well, the Nazis are animals, I'll give you that."

"They do seem to be lacking souls."

"Does Shroeder have all his marbles?"

"I believe he does."

"Why is Tolkien with him?"

"I'm afraid I'm to blame. I told him we wanted this abracadabra for ourselves."

"What are they up to?"

"I think they've set out to destroy the artifacts."

"Are we supposed to bring them back with their toys? Is that it?"

"That's the idea. Does Washington know you're here, by the by?"

"Afraid they'll steal the magic trinkets, are you?"

"It's England that's just a short boat ride from the continent," Fleming replied. "America won't be invaded any time soon. *Do* they?"

"No," Rex Dowling answered. "But I don't work for Washington. I work for one person in OSS."

"Does *he* know?"

"No. He just authorized me to help."

"Can he send more people?"

"No, we're it." Dowling nodded toward Hans and Jonas, who had not said a word. They watched as Hans smiled, and Jonas stood and walked over to a window. Soon they could hear the splash of his urine in the stream below.

"Can your man provide intelligence?" Fleming asked."

"Do you know the Three Kings Group, in Prague? František Moravec's outfit?"

"No."

"They know the Germans will be invading soon. They run recon flights across the border all the time. Very dangerous, as you can imagine."

"I can."

"All the pilots carry cyanide. A half dozen have not returned."

"Can they help?"

"They already have. They say there is a large Waffen unit, battalion strength, in the woods just west of the abbey."

"How many is that in Germany."

"The same as anywhere. Four to six hundred, maybe more."

"Christ."

"Yes, and they took pictures of recon foot patrols in all directions within a two-mile perimeter of the abbey."

"They must be wondering what's going on."

"They'll extract us if we need them to."

"We're a long way from that."

"Let me guess, you have no idea where Shroeder and Tolkien are?"

"And the dwarf."

"The dwarf?"

"Yes, Shroeder's valet. He's with them."

"A real dwarf?"

"It's a birth defect, Dowling."

"I know what it is."

Fleming smiled and put his hands up, palms forward, after saying this, a peace offering. He enjoyed teasing the American, but did not doubt his toughness. After all, he had just trekked two hundred kilometers to help out in a fight involving the four men in the mill against a Waffen SS battalion.

"Billie's with us," Fleming said, changing the subject, happy that Dowling had returned his smile. Their relationship would remain the same, even under stress. That was a good thing to know. "I'll be leaving to collect her."

"I thought as much," Dowling replied. "I saw her in town this morning."

"Saw her in town?" Fleming immediately regretted the precipitousness of this question.

"Yes," Dowling said. "Coming out of a chemist's."

Now Fleming remained silent. He had told Billie to stay in their room at the Hilltop Inn. Or had he just suggested it? She was a German citizen—not a Jew—free to wander about the country. They had made love all night and at six a.m. his head, well, it was filled with the scent and feel of her. He couldn't remember exactly what he had said.

"I decided to take a quick look," Dowling continued, eying Fleming a bit more carefully now, "to see if there were any Nazis about."

"I believe you're mistaken," said the Englishman.

Now it was Dowling's turn to pause. During this brief interval, Jonas returned to his place on the floor.

"Yes," Dowling replied at length, glancing casually at Hans and Jonas, "I may have been. The light was not good and I just caught a glimpse." The brothers remained silent, their faces passive, as if they were not interested in this part of the conversation.

Fleming was wearing a woolen sweater under a weather-beaten leather flyer's jacket and khaki field pants left over from his brief and unhappy matriculation at Sandhurst. On his feet were sturdy Alpine hiking boots. In the inside pocket of the silk-lined bomber jacket were his last pack of Morland's Specials. In his haste yesterday he had forgotten to take the carton from the drawer of his room's night table. He had forgotten his tortoiseshell holder as well. He wanted a Morland's now, badly, but did not reach for the pack. He stood up and glared at Dowling until the American looked away.

"Can you give me a description?"

"Two men—the two professors—both average height, one old with white hair, the other middle-aged. And a dwarf, redheaded, with a long braided red beard."

Dowling nodded, absorbing this information, then said, "Should they assist?"

"Yes, by all means."

"One more thing."

"Yes?"

The American pointed to the map. "This angel and dragon, what is it supposed to mean?"

"It's St. Michael slaying Satan. The abbey is officially called St. Michael's Abbey at Metten. Have you forgotten your Sunday School lessons, Dowling?"

Dowling smiled. "I suppose you had your own chapel on the manor grounds."

"We did."

"I skipped all that. I worked on Sundays."

"I see. Doing what?"

"Hawking newspapers, shoveling coal."

"How did you come to this?"

"We weren't allowed to take a paper home. They counted before and after. But before I turned my left-overs in, I read the whole edition, start to finish. It didn't take me long to figure out I could write a better news story than what they were printing. I applied when I was fifteen and they took me on, running copy. Now here I am."

"And OSS?"

"I got bored. I knew a guy who knew a guy. And you?"

"I lost a bet."

"Lost a bet?"

"Yes, I'll tell you about it someday. I'm off."

* * *

"What do you think, Hans?" Dowling said to the one-eyed brother after Fleming left.

"It was Miss Lillian."

"And this magic ritual?"

"I wore a St. Michael medal all through the war. They told us the English and the French were the devil."

"Did they tell you how to get in touch with him? We may need him after all is said and done."

Hans' reply was a shrug and an attempt at a wry smile, not easy with a cicatrix covering half his face.

"Jonas?" Dowling said.

"It was her."

"And the magic? Can it be real?"

The brothers shrugged in unison.

"We want to kill Nazis," Hans said, his smile gone. "Show us the way."

34.

Metten Abbey
October 8, 1938, 5:00 p.m.

"I lied to the lieutenant."

"Absolvo te."

"There is no tunnel here, but there is one just a hundred meters away, just south of our orchard, near the Roman wall."

"I see. What are they looking for, Father?"

"The tunnel leads to a small meadow, with sheer rock walls on all sides."

Father Wilfrid and Father William were sitting across from each other on rough-hewn but sturdy ladder-back chairs in Father William's cell located on the top floor front of Metten Abbey. The room's single twenty-four-inch by twenty-four-inch leaded glass window was a square blaze of bright yellow sunshine, a portal to heaven just above their heads as it were, that they might, if they only could, slip through, leaving Nazi Germany and the woes it had brought on their tonsured heads behind forever.

"How do you know this?" Father Wilfrid, the younger man by thirty years, asked.

"One of our monks took me there. Father Adelbert."

"When?"

"Soon after I arrived."

"In 1872?"

"Yes. I was seventeen."

"Why?"

"He told me he had been working in the archives, researching manuscripts over a thousand years old. He came upon a canto that, that . . ."

"Yes, that what?"

"That called upon Satan."

"Called upon Satan?"

"Yes, and that he had found an amulet in the forest, a black stone beast with ruby eyes that was spoken of in other manuscripts. That with the canto and the amulet he could . . ."

"He could what?"

"He could raise the dead."

The abbot realized deep in his soul, and with a sick feeling in his stomach that went far beyond mere nausea, that the tingling of the hair at the back of his neck and the sudden sweat on his brow were signs from God that the old priest sitting across from him was telling the simple, but horrific, truth. Despite this message from his soul, Father Wilfrid took a moment to look carefully into Father William's eyes. *It cannot be, dear Lord,* he murmured, *please take this from us.* Raising the dead? Only Christ, or Satan, could do that. But the old man's blue eyes were clear and calm, tinged only with the sadness of this burden he had been carrying for three quarters of a century. He was the sanest, the most even tempered of all the monks in the abbey. *I am sorry I doubted you, Lord,* the abbot said to himself.

"What happened to him?" Father Wilfrid asked. "Father Adelbert."

"No one knows. A few weeks after he showed me the walled meadow he disappeared."

"Disappeared?"

"He was seen in the kitchen yard one morning playing with Bridget, the yard dog, and then he was never seen or heard from again."

"Was there a search? His family?"

"He had no family. There was a search. He was never heard from again."

"Did you tell the abbot about the tunnel?"

"No. We were forbidden to leave the grounds. I was afraid I would be expelled. I wanted to serve God. I sinned."

"So this walled meadow was never searched."

"No."

"You have not sinned, Father."

"I would like you to hear my confession," said Father William.

"That's why I interrupted your day."

"I . . ."

"That's the excuse I gave the guard at your door."

"Ah, yes."

Coming through the window they now heard the chanting of the fourteen-hundred-year-old service that marked the beginning of vespers, the evening prayer.

Domine, ad adiuvandum me festina. Gloria Patri, et Filio, et Spiritui Sancto. Sicut erat in principio, et nunc et semper, et in saecula saeculorum. Amen. Alleluia. O God, come to my assistance. O Lord, make haste to help me • • •

In the good weather, the chapel doors, two stories below them, were swung open to make it easier for God and all of the angels, archangels, and saints in heaven to hear the evening prayer, a prayer of supplication and gratitude for the day that was coming to an end. In recent years, seeing what Hitler and his madmen were doing, Father Wilfrid had sometimes despaired that God was listening to any of his prayers. He hoped He was listening now.

The priests looked up at the glowing window and listened for a moment, then turned to face each other. "Bless me, Father, for I have sinned," said Father William.

35.

The Oder River
October 8, 1938, 7:00 p.m.

"Can it be?" the passenger in the Aero A14, whose name was Vaclav, but who called himself, deprecatingly, King Number One, said. He had lowered his binoculars to yell at the pilot in the open cockpit in front of him over the roar of the ancient bi-plane's engine.

"Can it be *what*?" the pilot, a nineteen-year-old aristocrat who had learned to fly at a rich man's flying club at a private airfield outside Prague, yelled back.

"At three o'clock," said Vaclav, "I saw something flashing a few miles up a tributary. Then I saw people in a clearing. I think the small ones had beards."

The boy pilot banked and descended. They had been cruising at two-thousand feet and would soon be at an altitude of only five hundred feet, close enough for the old bi-plane's Fairchild K19 aerial recon camera bolted to its belly—a gift from Vaclav's British friends—to take amazingly clear photographs. They were heading away from the setting sun, with a clear view of the earth below, but they saw nothing but the surprisingly wide tributary of the Oder as it glistened a dark green-brown in the last slanting light of the day. That and thick forest on either side.

"There was more than one small one?" the pilot said.

"Yes."

"This tributary is not on the map," the pilot said.

"It's an old map."

"Yes, or a new tributary."

"There, at one o'clock," Vaclav said, "There they are."

"I see nothing but water and trees."

"I'll be leaving you," Vaclav said, reaching to the floor at his feet for his parachute.

"What?"

"Crisscross this area taking pictures," Vaclav said. "Note your position. Tell Frantisek to expect to hear from me."

"Have you jumped before?"

"No, but it doesn't seem difficult."

"I will ascend first."

King Number One, age thirty-four, and with less than four years left to live, was already halfway out of his seat. After putting on his parachute, he reached to the floor again and pulled up the bulky rucksack containing a two-way radio similar to the one MI-6 had given Ian Fleming. This he strapped to his chest.

"Go at my signal," the young pilot said, holding his right thumb up and then closing it back into his fist. "I will level off. Count to three, then pull the cord."

As the plane rose they both looked below. There was no sign of the two professors and the red-bearded dwarf they had been instructed to be on the look-out for. Nor of any clearing. Neither spoke of the forest of tall trees that spanned the earth below as far as the eye could see. Only bad things, the least of which might be broken limbs, could happen from landing in one of them.

When the pilot gave him the thumbs up, Vaclav, who now had one leg out of his co-pilot's seat, smiled, returned the gesture, stepped out onto the bi-plane's lower wing, and leapt. He was carrying two CZ 27 semi-automatic pistols on his service belt and twenty extra clips in the pockets of his leather flight jacket.

Although he had been in airplanes many times, he had never jumped out of one. His two partners in the unit they called the Three Kings had been to jump school, but he had been traveling around Germany at the time as a ball bearing manufacturer's representative and had had to give that training a miss. No need to go into all that with the pilot.

In open space, watching the light-blue painted plane banking away, Vaclav continued smiling. He counted quickly to three and pulled the cord on his parachute. When the chute was open and he was drifting to earth, he gripped the radio to his chest, freed one hand, and waved goodbye to the young boy who he was fairly certain he would never see again.

36.
Metten Abbey
October 8, 1938, 7:00 p.m.

"You are lucky you weren't shot," said Kurt Bauer.

"I don't understand, Kurt," Billie Shroeder replied. "I am worried about my father. This was a logical place to look. I expected to find you here. I *hoped* to find you here, actually. Is my father here?"

"No, he is not," the young lieutenant replied.

Ian Fleming looked at Bauer's face, at his cold blue eyes, at the thin line of his mouth. *He wants her to call him lieutenant,* he thought. *And lover as well, I'll bet.*

He and Billie were standing in the abbey's vaulted entry hall. The Waffen corporal who had, at Billie's fierce insistence, called from the front gate to tell Bauer that Fraulein Lillian Shroeder, his old college chum, was asking to be admitted, stood off to the side. Two Waffen privates, machine guns unslung, stood on either side of them. Bauer, in a Waffen SS black waist jacket, his Walther P38 in a leather case on his web belt, faced them. In his officer's jodhpurs and shiny black boots, the lieutenant looked to Fleming every bit the iconic image of the German menace that would soon be unleashed on Europe: young, humorless, fanatic, soulless, eager to kill. If *these* warriors, these *creatures*, could be raised from the dead, then in a few years, all of Europe, and perhaps the world, would be on its knees before Adolph Hitler.

Out of the corner of his eye, Fleming saw a door open and a tonsured priest in a simple brown habit come out. He was relieved to have something else to think about. Whose side was this priest on?

"May I be of assistance?" the priest said, joining them, "I am the abbot here."

"You said the SS would not be involved," Billie said to Bauer, ignoring the priest. "There were troops at the front gate."

"They are here to help me search. Tolkien is missing as well. I believe they are . . ."

"They are *what*, Kurt?" Billie said. "My father is a German citizen, not a criminal."

Bauer looked from face to face, then said to the two guards, "You are dismissed."

When the guards were gone, Father Wilfrid introduced himself to Fleming and Billie, shaking Fleming's hand and nodding in deference to the beautiful Lillian Shroeder. "Can I offer you food or drink?" he said. "Or beds for the night?"

"No, you cannot," said Bauer. Then to Billie, "Where are you staying?"

"At the Hilltop Inn," Billie answered. "Just outside Deggendorf."

"In separate rooms, of course," said Fleming, his eyes twinkling. "By the way, Bauer, you don't happen to have a cigarette handy by any chance, do you? Terrible habit."

The young German officer looked at Fleming like he was insane.

"Father?" Fleming said.

"No, Mr. Fleming, I'm afraid not."

"Any chance you can hear my confession?"

"Are you serious?"

"Yes, couldn't be more serious."

"Lieutenant?"

"No. Absolutely not. He and Miss Shroeder are leaving."

"You can go to St. Peter's in Deggendorf," Father Wilfrid said. "Father Schneider hears confessions every Saturday night until seven-thirty. I will call him and tell him you are coming."

"Thank you, Father. You are very kind."

* * *

"Are you really going to confession?" Billie said. They were in the car on the way back to Deggendorf. Fleming was driving.

"Yes," he replied. Then, handing her a small piece of paper folded in half, he said, "Here, look at this." Billie took the two-inch by two-inch piece of lined notepaper, the kind a schoolboy might use, unfolded it, and read what was written there.

"What does it say?"

"It says, *we need to talk.* Where . . . ?"

"Did I get it?"

"Yes. Who . . ."

"Father Wilfrid."

"Tonight?"

"Yes, when we shook hands."

"He was taking an awful chance. What if you had been searched?"

"Nothing to it. I carry those little notes around all the time."

Billie smiled. "Are you even Catholic?" she asked.

"Tonight I am."

"But . . . Is that why you asked to have your confession heard?"

"Yes, course. He's a quick thinker, our Abbot Wilfrid. He will relay his message to Father Schneider. Perhaps our abbot has a bit of the spy in him. We shall see. By the way, old girl, Dowling said he saw you in town this morning, bright and early."

"*Did* he."

"Yes."

"He can be difficult, no? He was quite opposed to us visiting the abbey."

"I think he's got a crush on you."

155

"Are you jealous?"

"A little."

"First Kurt and now Dowling. But it's you I love. Do you love me?"

"I do."

"Even if I went into town this morning against your wishes?"

"That depends."

"On what?"

"Your reason for going."

"For this," Billie said, smiling. She had pulled a slender box, tied with a red ribbon, out of her purse.

"What is it? A pen?"

"Shall I open it?"

"Please."

Billie undid the ribbon, opened the box, and, using thumb and forefinger, took out a tortoiseshell cigarette holder. She smiled a wide, beautiful smile, a smile that men would cross oceans to see if it were meant for them.

"I bought you some cigarettes, too," she said. "A special blend. I know how you like to smoke after . . ."

"Yes," Fleming said, smiling. "I do. Thank you, my dear Billie."

37.
Berlin
October 8, 1938, 10:00 p.m.

Reinhard Heydrich stood at the tall window behind
his desk in his large and airy office at Gestapo Headquarters on Albrechtstrasse. There was no view here,
just the building across the street where a hundred
clerical drones worked to create the records necessary
to keep track of his secret police's doings. All of its
windows were ablaze. In his right hand were three
such documents. Behind him spread out on his desk
was a topographical map of Germany. He had read the
documents and now slowly read them again. The first
was a telegram from Lazarus, received at 8:00 a.m.
today. It simply said in plain text: HILLTOP INN
DEGGENDORF. The second was from Lieutenant
Bauer, a coded telex from Metten Abbey, decoded by
his staff: MISS SHROEDER AND FLEMING IN
DEGGENDORF WHAT ORDERS NO SIGN
OF QUARRY. The last was the most intriguing. It
was another coded telex, from another mole, the one
who went regularly to Goering's absurd parties in the
Brandenburg Forest:

> CHAOTIC SCENE HERE
> WHEN SMOKE BOMB (?) SET
> OFF LAST NIGHT. MANY
> SICK PARTY MEMBERS.

RUMOR THAT TWO OF HG'S PET DWARFS ESCAPED. ALSO RUMOR THAT TWO FAMOUS PROFESSORS AND THEIR DWARF VA-LET WERE HERE AND ARE MISSING. TONIGHT'S PAR-TY CANCELLED. RETURN-ING BERLIN.

Heydrich turned and bent over the map, where Carinhall was marked with a red pin and Metten Abbey with a green pin. The distance between them, some five hundred kilometers, he had calculated ear-lier. His traced his index finger between the two pins and asked himself again, why north? Then he spotted the gentle curve in blue ink of the Oder River and followed it first with his eyes and then with the same index finger. *Could they?* He thought. *Is it possible?*

38.
The Oder River
October 8, 1938, 10:00 p.m.

Professor Tolkien did not know for sure if the two young people who were by turns poling and rowing the raft were male or female. Indeed, they may not have been young. Their faces were smooth and their complexions flawlessly white, almost translucent, but their eyes were dark and without mirth, neither young nor old. They concentrated on the river ahead, and sometimes behind, with such intensity that the Englishman felt they could see not only the river's rippling black surface, but beneath it as well. In the middle of the large, flat vessel, the three dwarfs sat facing each other in a huddle, their heads down, their incongruously large hands wrapped around their knees. Like sleeping birds, Tolkien had said to himself when they assumed this position shortly after boarding. We don't like traveling by boat, Korumak had said just before they all nodded off more or less at the same moment. At the stern, under a brown tarp, lay the man whom Tolkien had first met near the top branches of a thick old oak tree some three hours ago. Vaclav, he called himself, "or King Number One, if you wish to be formal."

Franz Shroeder sat opposite, his back, like Tolkien's, leaning against the stabilizing, strapped-on steel drums that formed a low wall port and starboard.

They were all—except for Vaclav, who was in Czech Army fatigues and a severely battered leather bomber jacket—dressed in their woolen forest garb, their hoods up. The raft and its eight occupants formed the lowest, darkest possible profile against the night sky. The two sailors, who had been introduced by Trygg Korumak simply as his river dwelling friends, seemed to know where the current closest to the eastern bank was. All night they had avoided the main channel in the middle of the dark and mysterious Oder.

A rusted freighter going north had loomed ahead of them an hour earlier, forcing them to veer to the bank and take cover under the branches of the willows growing there in astonishing abundance. As the hulking freighter passed, perhaps fifty meters away, the sailing brothers—he assumed they were brothers because they looked so much alike—whispered to each other and nodded. After it passed they pushed away and resumed poling southward.

As the raft nudged along, Tolkien looked up for a bit, watching the half moon appear at intervals between scudding clouds. He should have been exhausted but he wasn't. They had walked for twenty hours through dense forest, with only the shortest of rest breaks at the longest of intervals, and reached a gnarled old oak tree with three trunks by the side of a small stream that fed into a short but wide tributary of the Oder at about 7:00 p.m. "We will wait here," Gylfi, who had led them with steady and unerring feet on their long journey, had said. But before they could settle down to rest and wait, they had heard an airplane overhead and dove for cover. A few minutes later came the sound of something crashing into the top of the triple-trunked oak. And then, astonishingly, a man's voice saying, *I need a knife*.

As he watched the moon and rehearsed the day's events, the English professor retrieved the last hunk of the dark brown bread—dwarf bread he had come to call it—that Dagna had given him, and began nibbling at it, marveling once again at its rough texture and oddly pleasing sweet and salty taste. As he ate, he noticed one of the sailing brothers looking at him. Without thinking he broke off a piece of the bread and offered it to the boy, who took it and swallowed it in one gulp and then smiled, a first.

Still smiling, the boy reached inside his shirt and handed something wrapped in bright red cloth to the Englishman, who took it and asked, "What is it?"

"Honey wafers," the boy said.

Tolkien unwrapped the wafers, broke a small piece off of one and ate it. *Goodness,* he said to himself, *this is not honey, it's nectar from Mount Olympus.* He ate more, then, encouraged, munching happily, he smiled back and said, "Thank you. This is delicious. What is your name?"

"I am called Talagan."

"And your brother?"

"He is called Narunir."

"Where are you from?"

"Where are we from?"

"Where do you live?"

"We live in the river."

In the river? Tolkien thought, and was about to say, you mean *on* the river, when Narunir tapped his brother on the shoulder from behind, and said, "It is safe, we will sail."

Tolkien leaned back and watched as the boys quickly stepped a mast that had been lying under a canvas cover in the center of the raft and let out a strange octagonal-shaped sail, also red. Talagan took the sheet while Narunir went aft and, stepping over the still sleeping Vaclav/King Number One, inserted a wooden rudder into a slot in the transom. Suddenly, with Narunir sitting on the raft's low transom, steering, and Talagan handling the sail, they were veering toward the middle of the river and making more headway than Tolkien, a landlubber, would have thought possible.

The cold breeze on his face and the swift movement of the raft were the last things the professor remembered before falling quietly and deeply asleep.

39.
Metten Abbey
October 8, 1938, 11:00 p.m.

"I just got off the phone with Heydrich."

"Yes, Reichsfuhrer."

"Do you have your map in front of you, Lieutenant? The standard issue topo of Germany?"

"No, Reichsfuhrer."

"Get it, please, and open it."

"Yes, Reichsfuhrer."

Lieutenant Kurt Bauer had had a long day, topped off, or so he thought, by the surprise visit of Billie Shroeder and the English reporter, Ian Fleming. There had been something odd about that visit, an undercurrent he could sense but did not understand. He had no qualms about letting them roam around Deggendorf. He trusted Billie. Not Fleming of course, but Billie, yes, she could be trusted. He needed to speak to her, but that would not be easy to accomplish with the Englishman in tow. He had been contemplating sending a car for her on some pretext when Himmler rang through. *Now what?* He thought, as he spread his map on the rustic table he was using as a desk in the abbey kitchen.

"I have it, Herr Reichsfuhrer," he said.

"Do you see how far the Oder River is from Carinhall?"

"Carinhall?"

"Yes, northeast of Berlin, near Lake Wuckersee. Do you see it?"

"Yes, Reichsfuhrer."

"The river, do you see it?"

"Yes, Reichsfuhrer."

"Do you see its route? In the south it becomes the Neisse."

"Yes, Reichsfuhrer."

"Do you see where it ends?"

"Yes, Reichsfuhrer."

"Do you see how far that is from Prague?"

"Yes, Reichsfuhrer."

"Our two professors were last seen in Carinhall."

"Carinhall?"

"They are not heading your way, Lieutenant. They are heading to Prague, and from there to England."

"Yes, Reichsfuhrer."

"With the artifacts."

Bauer did not reply. Using a red pencil, he was circling the area on the map where the professors might cross into Czechoslovakia, trying to estimate the distance from Metten Abbey. He was distracted by a knocking on the kitchen's oaken door, blackened on his side by the smoke of a thousand years of fires in the massive fireplace behind him.

"Lieutenant?"

"Yes, Reichsfuhrer."

"Do you know that Goering hates me and Himmler?"

Bauer did not answer.

"Surely you know we took the SS from him?"

Silence.

"He will never forgive us. He wants desperately to regain the Fuhrer's favor."

"Yes, Reichsfuhrer."

"He will send a party out."

"Yes, Reichsfuhrer."

"If you see them, arrest them."

"Herr . . ."

"That is a direct order."

"Yes, Reichsfuhrer."

"You are engaged now in an action that could advance your career by many years. Do you understand, Lieutenant?"

"Yes, Reichsfuhrer."

"Good. I want you on the move tonight."

"Yes, Reichsfuhrer."

"Oh, and by the way, Lieutenant, there are likely two new members of the party, also dwarfs, a man and a woman. You are equal to the task of apprehending two flabby old men and three creatures under four feet tall, are you not, Lieutenant?"

"Yes, Reichsfuhrer."

"I want Shroeder alive, with the artifacts. The others you can kill. I will give you twenty-four hours."

"Yes, Reichsfuhrer."

Himmler rang off with a loud clack.

"*Come in*," Bauer yelled, realizing that the knocking had gotten louder and more insistent. The door swung open and Father Wilfrid stepped in.

"Yes?" Bauer said, his volume lowered, but his voice sharp.

"Father William has died," the abbot said. "We will need permission to leave the abbey tomorrow morning to bury him."

"You can leave the building and keep going to the North Pole for all I care," Bauer replied. "My men and I are leaving within the hour."

40.
The Oder River
October 9, 1938, 6:00 a.m.

Professor Tolkien, from his perch on a low perimeter wall, scanned the cave that he had been told by Trygg Korumak would be his home for the next thirteen hours. The shock of being *in* the Oder River, or rather under it, had worn off, but not completely. The sight before him was too strange. Fifteen minutes ago they had turned into what he thought was the mouth of a wide, flat stream as dawn was about to break, and within seconds had literally sailed down under the Oder into the largest, most immaculately habitable cave he could have ever conceived existed on the planet. It was roughly circular, about fifty or sixty feet in diameter, its walls and twenty-foot-high ceiling a smooth granite-like stone filled with thousands of tiny bits of quartz, from which reflected the light of a dozen fires burning brightly in alcoves evenly spaced along the perimeter. The fires reflecting on the quartz shards lit the entire cave with a warm, translucent glow, as if moonlight and sunlight were mixed together by gods or alchemists in proportions only they knew.

At his feet was a rectangular resting space, as it was called by Narunir, perhaps six feet by four feet, marked out by low rocks and containing a luxurious bearskin rug. Shroeder was asleep in his across the way. Vaclav, the man who had parachuted upon them yesterday, was sitting on his rug in his resting space next to Tolkien's, staring at the cave. At his feet were his radio, which he had been fidgeting with for the last twenty minutes, and a spread-out topographical map, with coordinates, of the Oder-Niesse River valley. The river-dwelling boys, the dwarfs trailing, had disappeared through an arched doorway. They had admonished them to rest, saying that they would soon bring food. The most astonishing things about the cave were the pools of water in its center, one steamy hot, the other ice cold, both surrounded by a smooth ledge of the same quartz-filled granite as the walls and ceiling. They had all used the hot water to clean their hands and faces when they first arrived, and drunk the cold water from wooden ladles laid out for them on the ledge. Off to the left, out of sight, the raft was beached on a scree of dry, sandy soil. Behind it, the stream they had sailed in on dipped under the cave, to emerge where, the professor could not guess. It could be heard coursing beneath the cave's flat, carpet-covered stone floor, as could the Oder be heard above. These were sights and sounds that no writer could ever dream of seeing. But here he was.

"I never got the chance to properly thank you for climbing that tree," said Vaclav, who had clambered onto the wall to sit next to the professor. "I would have thought one of those little monkeys would have done it."

"They don't like heights," Tolkien replied. "And I'd be careful calling them monkeys. They are astonishingly smart and brave."

"Sorry, no offense was meant. They *are* tiny, that's the thing." Vaclav stood over six feet tall himself.

"Their hearts are very large. They killed five Nazi soldiers in the forest yesterday with their axes."

"That warms my heart. Who were these Nazi fuckheads?"

"They were chasing us with a pack of hounds."

"What happened to the hounds?"

"They ran."

"They ran?"

"Yes."

"I see. You must tell me how you managed that."

"Perhaps someday I'll write about it."

"You're a writer?"

"A college professor."

"Where are we, Professor?"

"In a cave under the Oder River."

"I think it would be the Niesse by now."

"Likely. My geography is not as good as it might be. We traveled far last night. At least I think we did. I slept the whole time."

"Where are you going? One of the river boys said you were a '*fellowship*.' He used the word quite reverently, I might add. What did he mean?"

"I don't know," the professor replied, thinking, *then again, perhaps I do.*

"Where is this fellowship headed?" Vaclav asked.

"Tell me who *you* are first."

"I told you last night, I am a Czech Army captain, a ranger in a special unit. I sometimes assist in reconnaissance flights. The Germans have taken the Sudetenland without a fight, but from now on, we fight."

"A ranger?"

"We are shadow warriors, a special group, if you will."

"Spies?"

"If necessary. Were you in the war?"

"Yes, in France."

"It's coming again."

"Are you sure?"

"I've been all over Germany in the last five years. A war machine is being built like no other the world has ever seen. They will crush all of Europe in six months if we don't stop them."

"How did you know about us?"

"I was told to be on the lookout for two men and a dwarf. I did not think you would be so far north, but there you were, except you were two men and *three* dwarfs."

"What were you told about us?"

"That the Germans would kill you if someone didn't get to you first."

"Anything else?"

"That if you were spotted, I was to make sure you arrived safely in Prague, and with all deliberate speed. All of you."

"So you jumped."

"Yes. It was fun."

"It was fun? You mean you never jumped before?"

"No, but I've watched."

"Who *are* you?"

"I hate the Germans. That's all you need to know. Now tell me, who are *you*, really, and why are you running?"

41.

The Bavarian Forest, Near Deggendorf
October 9, 1938, 8:00 a.m.

"There's a priest at the bridge," said Jonas Kaufman. He was sitting on a three-legged stool at a window overlooking the stream and the old wooden bridge. "On a bicycle."

"Christ," said Rex Dowling, who was sitting nearby on the floor, the radio in front of him.

The others, Fleming, Billie, and Hans, were also sitting on the floor, eating their breakfast of thick and rich Irish porridge out of tins that Hans had taken from the Adlon's gloriously stocked kitchen before leaving Berlin. Spoons in one hand, tin cans of pre-cooked oatmeal in the other, they looked in unison at Jonas.

Fleming put his things down and scrambled to the window on all fours. "Let me see," he said, when he reached Jonas, indicating the binoculars that the German held to his eyes.

"Father Schneider," Fleming said after putting the glasses to his brow and adjusting the focus wheel slightly. "From St. Peters."

"The one who heard your confession last night?" Dowling asked.

"Yes. I told him if he heard anything else from the abbey to come to the mill."

"You told him where we were?"

"I had no choice."

"Does he look like he's carrying a weapon?"

"No."

"Where is he now?"

"On our side of the bridge."

"I will go," said Hans, who was already on his feet, his woolen cap on, his machine gun over his shoulder.

Fleming nodded, as did Dowling, who had crawled to the window and was peering out, concealing as much of himself as possible. They watched as Hans exited the mill through its large storage room door immediately below them and walked slowly toward the priest, who stopped and put his hands in the air when he spotted the one-eyed war veteran, who had unslung his weapon and was carrying it at the ready. Father Schneider kept his hands up as Hans came up to him. They spoke for a few seconds and then the priest, a small, thin man in spectacles, looked up at the mill's second floor windows. In one of them, the one next to Fleming and Dowling, knelt Jonas Kaufman, his rifle aimed at the cleric's chest.

"That's a professional search he's doing," Fleming said. Father Schneider was now kneeling, his hands clasped on top of his head, as Hans went about his business.

"Yes. He was in charge of French prisoners at the end of the war. He learned to be thorough."

"He won't do a cavity search, I hope," said Fleming. "The man is on our side."

"Probably not. But I think that he lost his eye doing a search. The POW had a razor blade in his teeth. Slashed him pretty good until another guard shot him."

"How do you know this?

"Rumor. Hans will say nothing."

"Here they come."

* * *

"Bauer and the troops are gone," said Father Schneider.

"What? Are you sure?" Fleming asked.

"Yes, I was at the abbey this morning to say mass. Father Wilfrid asked me to ride over to tell you."

"Are there none left?" Billie said.

"There is a group camped in the courtyard."

"How many?"

"Forty men."

"What happened?" Fleming asked. "Why did they leave?"

"I don't know. Father Wilfrid does not know."

"Where were they headed?"

"Father heard them say north."

"Do you think you were followed?"

"I rode here directly from the abbey. I was not followed."

"What else did Father Wilfrid say?" Fleming asked. "Did he tell you when they left?"

"They left last night, just before midnight."

The group was silent for a moment as they took this in. The priest, pale of face and shy, but obviously determined to carry out the abbot's request, sat before them on the three-legged stool. They had given him a tin cup of water, which he now sipped. "I must return soon," he said after lowering the cup. "We are burying Father William."

"The one who knew about the tunnel?" Fleming said.

"Yes, he died last night."

"How? Bauer?"

"No, he called for Father Wilfrid, said his confession, and died a moment later."

Fleming shook his head. At his faux confession last night, Father Schneider had relayed Abbot Wilfrid's terse message: *there is a tunnel entrance near a Roman wall one hundred meters south of our orchard. It leads to the Devil's Canyon.* That had been the first he had heard the term Devil's Canyon. He had been hoping to connect somehow with Father William to ask about it.

"The Devil's Canyon," Fleming now said. "What do you know about it."

"Nothing," the timid priest replied. "Rumors."

"What kind of rumors?"

"That one of the monk's made a pact with the Devil in a hidden canyon in the forest many years ago, a hundred years ago, no one knows when or who."

"Do you know where the tunnel entrance is?" Billie asked. "Does Father Wilfrid?"

"No, only Father William knew. He did not tell Father Wilfrid."

"Are you sure?" Dowling asked.

"Yes. Father urged him to tell, but he would not."

"Are the troops making patrols?" Dowling asked.

"Yes, Father said one group is circling the abbey at all times."

"One group? How many, did he say?"

"No, I'm sorry, just one group. They patrolled last night and Father Wilfrid believes they will patrol around the clock."

"Do they have a radio?"

"Yes, it is set up in the kitchen. A soldier stays with it."

"Does he have a replacement?"

"Yes, the Father said the sergeant relieves him."

"Are they sleeping in the courtyard?"

"Yes. I believe so. There are tents there and gear."

"Is there an officer?"

"No, just the sergeant. I do not know his name."

"Do they post lookouts?"

"I don't know,. Father did not say. We did not talk long. He walked me to the front gate. We talked as we walked. Or, rather, he talked, I listened."

"Are the gates guarded? When we visited there were troops outside the gates."

"Yes, four men."

"Are there gun placements? Machine guns set up?"

"I saw one in the tower."

"Who is feeding them?"

"Feeding them?"

"Yes."

"The machine guns?"

"No, the troops."

"Ah, the troops. The monks are."

"How do you know this?"

"Father asked me to bring back a sack of flour to make bread. He said they are feeding the soldiers and are running low."

"Do they have a regular cook?"

"Yes, Father Adam."

"When is meal time? When does Father Adam cook?"

"Six in the morning, noon, and six in the evening."

"The patrol, where do they eat?"

"I don't know."

"Do you know their schedule?"

"No, I just know that Father Wilfrid believes that they will patrol the grounds around the clock."

"How far out? What distance from the abbey?"

"I don't know. Please, I must go. I've told you everything."

"Go," said Fleming, extending his hand. The priest grabbed it and Fleming hoisted him gently from the stool.

"How can we contact Father Wilfrid?" Fleming asked.

"I will ride over for you. Just come to the rectory."

"What is your routine? Do you go on a regular schedule?"

"I go every Saturday afternoon to hear confessions. And when Father Wilfrid calls and asks me. He called this morning and asked me to come to assist him at mass and to help prepare Father William's body for burial."

"Thank you, Father," Fleming said. "You have been very helpful."

"Helpful with what?" the priest asked.

"Permit me to ask you a question first," said Fleming. "What is motivating you to help us? You are a German citizen. This is your country, those are German troops at the abbey."

"I am Austrian," Father Schneider replied. "Not German. I was born a Jew, orphaned when my parents were killed in a pogrom. I was taken in by the local Sisters of Mercy. They did not encourage me to convert. I insisted. I listen to the BBC every night in the rectory attic. The Nazis are killing Jews by the thousands, and soon, if they are not stopped, it will be in the millions. The Catholics will be next . . . I am both a Jew and a Catholic, a rarity, but here I am. So, Herr Fleming, what am I helping you with?"

"I will say only this, my dear Father," said Fleming. "The second world war in our lifetime has started, and you are on the right side."

* * *

"Can we take them by surprise?" said Dowling, when Father Schneider was gone. "It's forty against four."

"Five," Billie said. "You're not leaving me behind."

"Can you handle a weapon?" said Dowling.

"Yes. I was in a gun club in college. I was too old for Hitler Youth, and this was an acceptable alternative."

"Then you're coming," said Fleming. "It's *your* father after all."

"We will have to attack the patrol, plus the troops at the abbey," said Hans Kaufman. "With five people, it can't be done."

"We can disable the troops at the abbey," said Fleming.

"How do you propose to do that?" Dowling asked.

"Poison," Fleming replied. "We will poison the troops at the abbey and ambush the patrol."

"Poison," said Hans Kaufman. "Excellent."

"How?" Billie asked.

"In their food. Father Schneider will help us."

"We can't kill the radio operator," said Dowling.

"No, nor the sergeant," said Fleming. "We'll need them alive."

"Why?" Billie asked.

"In case Bauer checks in," Dowling replied.

"How will we get poison?" said Billie. "And what kind?"

"We will visit the chemist in town," Fleming answered, "and pick up the last things from our room, say goodbye to our lovely innkeeper."

42.
The Niesse River
October 9, 1938, 10:00 a.m.

"We are wasting time sitting here," Vaclav said.

"As I've said," Trygg Korumak replied. "We can only sail at night. There is too much activity on the river during the day."

"We are 190 kilometers from the Czech border," the Army captain said. "That will take three nights of sailing."

"What do you propose?"

"I need to leave the cave so I can use my radio. I can get a plane to pick us up and fly us to Prague, or Metten if you prefer."

Vaclav eyed Professor Tolkien as he said this.

"How do you know about Metten?" Korumak asked.

"I told him," said Tolkien.

The group was silent. They were sitting on the floor between the two pools. They had eaten honey cakes and bread and drank a tart beer-like drink, all produced by the river-dwelling brothers from the room beyond the arch, to which they had returned, leaving the three men and three dwarfs to discuss their business.

"How do we know he is who he says he is?" Korumak said finally.

"We have followed you here," Tolkien said. "We have trusted you and your friends. I now choose to trust our ranger captain as well."

"Does he know what our mission is?"

"Yes, I told him," Tolkien replied.

They now all turned to Franz Shroeder. He had said nothing. He was fingering the amulet through the spun woolen material at the front of his tunic. He remained silent, his thoughts seemingly elsewhere.

"How will you land a plane here?" Korumak asked.

"There are a half dozen possibilities nearby," Vaclav said. "My friends have flown in and out of tighter spots."

"And in Metten? How will we land there?" the dwarf asked. "There will be German soldiers everywhere."

"I daresay we'll jump," said Tolkien, unable to suppress a smile. Ever since Vaclav told him of his flight through the air of the evening before, he had been imagining what it would be like to float easily from on high, to land with a quiet thud in a farm field or on a leafy street in Oxford. *That* would surprise the neighbors.

"Yes," Vaclav answered, "we will, and it will have to be at night."

Professor Tolkien was the only one who had developed any rapport with Vaclav, whose main pleasures seemed to be to kill Nazis and to talk about killing Nazis. He looked around at the group now, knowing what he would see: the faces of the dwarfs white as ghosts. And that's exactly what he saw. They were brave men but they looked now like they were about to vomit.

"You can't be serious," said Korumak.

"I'll jump," Franz Shroeder said. "This man is right. We have to get to the abbey as quickly as possible."

"Professor . . ." Korumak said, but before he could say another word, Shroeder interrupted him.

"My dear Trygg, my faithful friend, you know more than anyone the weight I am carrying. You have known it for many years. I alone must carry it, but I cannot bear it much longer."

They all looked at Shroeder, who had seemed a different man since the episode in the forest. The raising of the amulet had nearly killed him, yet, afraid that more soldiers were on their trail, they had had to push on, dragging and carrying the old man through dense forest to their rendezvous with the river dwellers. He had slept on the raft and all morning in the cave, fourteen hours in all, and had eaten and drunk with the rest of them, but still he looked worn and haggard.

"It's settled, then," said Vaclav. He rose and picked up the rucksack containing his radio.

"Wait," said Korumak. "Talagan or Narunir will have to take you out and back."

"I can find my way."

"No, you can't," said Talagan, who was now standing in the arched doorway. "It is forbidden."

"What is forbidden?" the Czech asked.

"For anyone to enter or exit this river dwelling except in the presence of a river dweller."

"River dweller?" said Vaclav. "You are boys who have found a cave."

"You must cooperate, my dear captain," said Tolkien. "These boys, these dwarfs, they are not what you think they are. There is a war coming, and we will need their help to win it."

43.

**The Bavarian Forest, Near Deggendorf
October 9, 1938, 2:00 p.m.**

"What did you get?" Rex Dowling asked.

"Rat poison," Ian Fleming replied. "We delivered it to Father Schneider and came right here."

"What did you tell him?"

"To wait for word from us."

"You better go back and tell him to deliver it now, to be served à la carte at tonight's dinner."

"What? Why?"

"A message came through from the Three Kings in Prague. Our boys are being dropped tonight in a field near the abbey."

"Dropped? Where are they?"

"Somewhere north on the Niesse River. One of Moravec's men found them. He made contact today, asked for a plane to pick them up and take them to Metten."

"Do you have the coordinates?"

"Yes, a field about two miles east of the abbey. They'll be dropping them tonight at ten or so. They have taken on some help, two men, two *small* men to be precise, plus Moravec's man."

"What were they doing up north."

"I wasn't told."

"Do they know we'll be meeting them?"

"Yes."

179

"It's settled," Fleming said without hesitation, "the good padre must deliver the rat poison this afternoon. I'm sure they can use another sack of flour at the abbey. Billie, can you ride over to tell him? I've shown my face enough in Deggendorf. I'll stay and help get ready."

"Yes," Billie said. "Of course. It will be a pleasure."

"Rat poison," Dowling said. "Appropriate. Will it kill them?"

"We told the chemist we needed to kill a dozen big rats," Billie answered. "He said what he gave us would do the trick. It's arsenic, basically, in a white powder. It causes massive internal hemorrhaging. They may not die immediately, but they will be on their backs very quickly, in agony."

"Let's kill them all," said Hans Kaufman. "I can operate the radio."

<u>44.</u>
Over The Niesse River Valley
October 9, 1938, 8:15 p.m.

"Why can't we land in Metten?" Trygg Korumak asked.

"The pilot does not know the terrain," Vaclav replied. "It will be dark. This plane needs a lot of runway. We have to jump."

"How high are we?"

"Do you really want to know?"

"Ten feet or ten thousand feet, I'm in the air, it doesn't matter."

"We're at fifty-one hundred feet," Vaclav replied, after glancing at the altimeter.

Korumak and Vaclav were in the stripped down Avia 158's cockpit. Vaclav, in the co-pilot's seat, had to twist around and look down at Korumak, who was sitting on the floor just behind him over the hinged sheet metal door that they would be jumping out of in two hours. The plane had no actual jump door as the pilot and co-pilot would jump from the cockpit doors if and when they had to eject. A mechanic had hurriedly jerry-rigged this door in the floor that afternoon. Vaclav and Korumak were shouting at each other over the roar of the plane's twin engines. In the fuselage, sitting hands to knees, were the rest of the fellowship of six, as Tolkien had dubbed them. The pilot, grinning happily, was the same boy who had dropped Vaclav the night before. "My king," he had said, as he greeted his countryman in the potato field he had landed in almost precisely on time at eight o'clock.

"We will jump together," Vaclav said. "Just hug me tight and hold on. Think of me as a beautiful woman that you are madly in love with. When we hit the ground, it will be orgasmic."

* * *

In the rear, there was no banter. Professor Tolkien and Professor Shroeder, their chutes strapped to their backs, sat next to each other, leaning against the hull. Directly across sat Gylfi and Dagna, their faces pasty white. They were afraid of heights and afraid of jumping, and the loud, bumpy ride did not help.

"Are you alright, Franz?" Tolkien asked.

"It's almost done," the German professor replied.

"The flight? No, we just took off."

"Not the flight. Our journey."

"The ritual?"

"Yes. I am being drawn like a magnet."

"Tell me about it."

"It's simple. I pile kindling around the base of the Devil's Oak. I light the kindling. I kneel at the black stone alter. I recite the *Vedo* until the tree is fully in flames. I throw the parchment and the amulet into the flames."

"You will need help," said Tolkien.

"I took the amulet and the parchment from Father Adelbert's dead body. I unleashed this evil. I must destroy it."

"Yes, but Professor, you say the tree is a hundred feet tall, the trunk ten feet in diameter. It will not burn. You will need fuel, not just kindling."

"Petrol, perhaps," said Shroeder.

"How will we get it?"

"Not petrol, lamp oil," Shroeder replied. "The monks use it at the abbey."

"You mean when you were a student?"

"Yes."

"But that was sixty years ago."

"The monks throw nothing away."

"How will we get it?"

"I don't know. But we will."

"Do you know where the tunnel entrance is?"

"Yes, I will find it."

"I will go down with you."

"Where do the monks keep the lamp oil?" asked Dagna.

"You have been listening," said Shroeder.

Dagna nodded, as did Gylfi.

"In a large store room next to the kitchen," Shroeder replied. "There is a large drum and tins for pouring."

"We'll get the oil," said Dagna.

"And we'll go with you into the canyon," said Gylfi.

"God be with us," said Tolkien.

45.

Metten Abbey
October 8, 1938, 8:15 p.m.

"Are they dead?" Fleming asked.

"Yes," Rex Dowling replied.

The Englishman and the American, their faces blackened with soot scraped from the interior walls of the mill's crumbling fireplace, were standing over the bodies of four Waffen-SS troops lying on the ground along the five-foot-high stone wall that stretched out on either side of Metten Abbey's filigreed wrought iron front gate. A fire blazed in a two-hundred-liter steel drum a few feet away. Tin mess kits littered the ground near the drum.

The small party of four men and Billie had waited until nightfall to make the two-mile hike through the forest to the abbey. It had been very slow going as they were constantly stopping to listen for the German patrol. When they got near the front gate, Fleming and Dowling, the group's de facto, unspoken co-leaders, had told the Kaufmans and Billie to stay in the darkness of the tree line while they approached.

Now Fleming put two fingers to his mouth and let out a short, shrill whistle. He counted to ten and did it again. He and Dowling watched as Hans, Jonas and Billie, all in rough gear, their faces blackened as well, all carrying machine guns, approached them at a crouching run.

"They're dead," he said when they reached the wall. "Take their weapons and ammo, scatter them. Hans, Jonas, drag the bodies into the woods."

"What now?" Billie whispered.

"The machine gun," said Fleming.

"He should be dead too," said Dowling.

"One can only hope," said Fleming, smiling. "Nevertheless, we'll go around back."

As Hans and Jonas were returning from dumping the bodies, the sound of the abbey's front door swinging open could be distinctly heard. Dowling got down on all fours and crawled to the corner where the foot of the gate joined the wall.

"It's a priest," the American said, "and a soldier with a gun at his head."

Fleming crawled over to have a look at the scene perhaps thirty yards away. "Christ," he said. "It's Father Wilfrid."

"*Unteroffizier, sind sie da?!*" the soldier at the door shouted.

"*Ja, Stabsunteroffizier, komm,*" Fleming replied.

"Frederick?"

"*Ja, komm. Wir sind erbrochenes.*"

"He's not coming," said Dowling. "It must be your accent. No *unteroffizier* sounds like an English toff. You don't sound sick either."

Before Fleming could answer, a shot rang out, the sergeant's head exploded and he crumpled to the ground. Father Wilfrid stood frozen in place. This tableau, Fleming and Dowling, still crouching, hidden behind the wall, could plainly see in the light spilling out through the abbey's wide open front door.

"Who in hell?" Fleming asked and then he had to duck and pull back as machine gun fire from the abbey began peppering the wall to his left, where, come to think of it, he said to himself, the shot that had felled the German sergeant had come from. He looked that way and saw Hans and Jonas crouching behind the wall, their heads together. Billie was crouching next to them. Fleming caught her eye and waved her over. Covered by the wall, she ran to his position. The machine gun fire had stopped but now began again, this time strafing along the top of the wall as if the gunner could see or sense Billie running behind it. Fleming ducked low and took a look through the gate up at the tower, where he could see the muzzle flashes of the machine gun in a turret window on the second floor. Father Wilfrid was kneeling over the German sergeant.

A movement to Fleming's left caught his eye. Looking that way he saw Jonas leap over the wall and run full out to a tree about twenty yards away on the lawn that bordered the courtyard. When he got there, he crouched and raised his right arm. At this signal Hans stood and began firing his machine gun up at the turret window. Under this covering fire, Jonas stepped out and flung a hand grenade up at the turret. It hit the wall beneath the window and blasted away a ragged chunk of it. Hans was still firing non-stop. Jonas pulled another grenade off of his shoulder clip and flung it, this time directly into the turret window, where it exploded, sending rock and glass and the German gunner's body flying through the air.

"He must not have been hungry," said Fleming.

"Look," Dowling said. "The priest."

They peered through the clearing smoke and saw Father Wilfrid staggering toward them, a huge bloody gash where his face should have been. He took one last step, reached his hand out, and slumped to the ground.

"Hans," Fleming said. "Cut the telephone lines."

46.
The Bavarian Forest
October 8, 1938, 8:30 p.m.

"We're *here*," said Dowling.

The group was huddled in a grove of tall fir trees about a mile east of the abbey. Dowling's flashlight shone on a map he had unfolded and placed on the needle-covered forest floor.

"We have ninety minutes," said Fleming.

"Will we make it?" Billie said.

Dowling ran the end of the narrow beam of the flashlight along the course they would take to get to the landing field, which he had marked in red before leaving the mill. "It's four-plus miles," he said. "It'll be close."

Knowing that the firefight would surely draw the German patrol back to the monastery, Fleming and Dowling had decided that the best thing to do was to head posthaste to the landing field. They knew that when the patrol arrived at the abbey, the lives of all of the monks would be in grave danger. The machine gunner dead from a grenade attack, the rest of the troops either dead or deadly sick. Whoever was in charge would have to improvise. Hopefully the first thing he did was to get rid of the leftover poisoned food and spirit away the cook whose work it was. The cook and Father Schneider were dead men if they were discovered, but there was no help for that now.

Fleming and the American had agreed that the less they knew at the abbey, the better, especially when it came to their numbers and the direction they were heading.

"We need to push on," said Fleming. "Single file, as quietly as possible. I don't think the patrol will set out for us. There are only eight of them and they don't know where to begin to look. But we can't be sure, so it's quiet, deliberate speed."

"Surely they'll do something," said Billie.

"They'll radio for help," said Dowling, but as far as I know the nearest army base is outside Stuttgart, that's about two hundred miles. My estimate is that we have about four hours to collect your father and his party, bring them to the magic canyon and get us all to safety."

"What's the plan for that?" Billie asked.

"I don't know."

"Neither do I," said Fleming, "but it's early, we'll figure something out."

<u>47.</u>
Above The Bavarian Forest
October 9, 1938, 10:15 p.m.

The field was much bigger than either Vaclav or the pilot thought it would be from looking at the map. Marked out, as requested, by bonfires at either end, it was perhaps a quarter mile in length and looked as if someone had tried to grow crops in it at one time. The light from the half moon was so good that the bonfires were not really needed. But that chance could not be taken. In the pilot's experience, clouds flew around the night sky on schedules only they knew for sure.

On their first descent they had seen a much smaller cleared area and the outline of a dilapidated farmhouse. The pilot now descended again and circled the field. He was, Vaclav knew, ready to drop his human cargo.

"All ready, my king?" the pilot said to Vaclav.

"Yes."

"I will come in from the east, the wind will blow you back a bit."

"Fine."

"By the way, I can land here."

"You can? Then land for God's sake. Do the dwarfs and the two professors a favor."

"I can't now, fuel." The young flier pointed to the fuel gauge on the instrument panel. It read empty. "I think it's wrong, but you're safer to jump."

"Fuck."

"It's this plane. It's a prototype, one of a kind. Rejected by the air force for many reasons."

"Leaky fuel tanks among them."

"I hope not. I have a hot date tonight. Hate to let her down."

"If you make it back to Prague, can you come back to pick us up?"

"Of course. What time?"

"What about your date?"

"War is hell."

"Say o-one hundred."

"Fine."

"I don't know about the bonfires."

"I'll find it."

Vaclav nodded. Where did these kids come from? God knows we'll need them when the Germans invade.

* * *

The pilot banked and leveled off at a thousand feet, heading due east. The forest below, dense and black, whizzed by for a few seconds and then, about a quarter mile from the edge of the field, he raised his thumb to Vaclav. The English professor was sitting on the edge of the jump door. Vaclav nodded to him and raised his thumb and the professor jumped. In a line facing Vaclav the others waited their turn. The German professor was next. His long white hair blew wildly in the wind from the open door. He crouched and sat for a second on the door's rim, then slipped away into the night.

The pilot turned to check his instruments. The fuel gauge still read empty. He was certain that he had not miscalculated his flight time or rate of consumption. Fairly certain. A moment later he heard Vaclav say, "hold on tight, we're off." The pilot kept his heading but began to climb, happily, into the cloud cover that was beginning to amass. He would have to cross the rest of Germany and then the Ger-man-occupied Sudetenland before he could breathe easily. Before entering the clouds, he banked slightly to the left, turned and looked down, and saw a line of five parachutes in perfect formation drifting down toward the field.

48.
The Bavarian Forest
October 9, 1938, Midnight

A checkerboard pattern of clouds drifted by above the heads of the six people sitting near Metten Abbey's orchard wall. The moonlight that broke through at eerily regular intervals cast its silver light on their faces at the same intervals—the grim, tired faces of one woman and five men. The ground floor lights in the abbey were on, but they neither saw nor heard any movement. Guided by Trygg Korumak, who seemed to know the area intimately, they had made their way from the drop area through a deep pine forest, made deeper by the failure of any moonlight to penetrate the dense canopy that loomed overhead, as if, they all felt, they were hiking through a living, breathing tunnel.

The other five members of the fellowship, as Professor Tolkien had come to describe it to himself, were off on missions: the Kaufman brothers to scout the Roman wall, and the three dwarfs to steal lamp oil from the abbey.

What else but a fellowship? Tolkien said to himself. A fellowship whose oath had been sworn not with words, but with deeds: the escape from Carinhall, the slaying of the German soldiers hunting them, the leap from an airplane into the abyss of the night, the trek through forest, after the firefight at the abbey, by virtual strangers to collect other virtual strangers in a godforsaken farm field. Who needs to swear an oath after doing such things?

The English professor was sitting off to the side, perhaps twenty feet from the others. He did not expect to survive the night, which was too bad. He had been feeling low of late for reasons he could not fathom, unable to write, at odds with his publisher, tired of lecturing to teenage boys who were passionate about all the wrong things, detached from life. Now all was clear, especially the confusion that had been dogging him about the novel he was writing. *Good-evil, honor-desecration, base-noble*—if he lived he would write about these things, with no fear or reservation, no self-doubt. Not after what he had seen in the last two days.

"Hello, professor," someone said. "Are you with us?"

"Yes, Fleming," Tolkien replied, "I'm with you."

"Good, you were drifting, exhausted I'm sure."

"No, exhilarated, actually."

"Exhilarated, well . . ."

"Did you want to speak to me?"

"Yes, before it's too late."

"You want me to lend you my years."

"Pardon?"

"Sorry, it's something I tell students who come to me."

"The letter," Fleming said, haltingly, "my father . . . Can you tell me now how and when you met him? Do you mind?"

Tolkien smiled. "You realize where we are, Fleming?" he said. "A distraction would be quite welcome."

Fleming looked discomfited, and Tolkien regretted his sarcasm. Mild though it was, it had plainly pierced his young countryman's emotional armor. Did this brash young fellow actually *have* a sensitive heart? And then Tolkien realized that brash and young, though often going nicely together in the same sentence, did not mean *immune to pain*. "Of course, my dear fellow," he said. The professor paused to gaze with new eyes on Fleming and then began.

"We landed in the same muddy shell crater one night during an assault. Your father's horse was badly injured, he was sprawled across your father's legs."

"When was this?"

"The Somme."

"Ah, he died the following May."

"Yes, I read about it and posted the letter."

"What did he talk about?"

"He berated me for sparseness of speech."

"Berated you . . . ?"

"Yes, but it was . . ." Here Tolkien paused again, remembering that night in 1916. "It was said from one soldier to another. A sort of . . . I was going to say camaraderie, but that's not what it was. It was more like older to younger brother, or father to son. Utterly respectful, mischievous actually, old Etonians and all that. I must say, if you will pardon my sentimentality, even *loving*. Of course in the most obscure of English ways. I offered to shoot the horse, but he did it himself."

"He loved horses, could never understand why I didn't," said Fleming.

"He was the bravest soldier I met in the war," Tolkien said, "and I met many brave ones, and many broken by cowardice as well."

Then Tolkien said what he thought he would never say to anyone. "I thought he was going to die. He ordered me to get back to the assault, not to come looking for him, an order that to this day I regret obeying."

"Why?"

"I was afraid, you see. No man's land . . . Had I gone back, his life might have been different. He might not have died in that farmhouse in Picardy."

"Nonsense."

"Before I left him I gave him my Benedict medal. I should have gone back, but . . . but . . ."

"*What* did you say? *What* did you give him?"

"The St. Benedict medal my wife gave me when I shipped out."

Fleming reached into his leather jacket, pulled out his wallet and carefully extracted from its secret pocket a St. Benedict's medal. "Is this it?" he said to Tolkien, handing the medal to him.

Tolkien took the medal, turned it over and ran his fingers over its smooth surfaces. "Where did you get this?" he said.

"It was in a leather pouch in my father's tunic. They sent it with the packet of his personal things. There was a note in the pouch as well."

"What did it say?"

"For Johnnie."

"You."

"Yes."

Through his blouse front Fleming fingered the replacement *Vedo* medal he had worn around his neck the past twenty-two years.

"Is it yours?" Fleming asked again.

"Of course," Tolkien replied. "Your father said his family was rather free-form when it came to religion, but the medal, well, it was the best I could do, knowing I wasn't going back to save him."

"You shall have it back."

"Nonsense," Tolkien replied, surprising himself by raising his voice and speaking sharply. "I have a replacement, given me by Edith. This medal is yours." He handed the *Vedo* back to Fleming, who took it without hesitation. "It was always meant to be for Johnnie," Tolkien said. "Indeed, perhaps for use this very night."

"Use? I'm not sure what you mean."

"It's not just the German army we'll be facing tonight, surely you understand that."

"I do, but . . ."

"*But?* Once the business in the canyon starts, you'll know instantly what I mean."

"But you can't . . ."

"I can't what?"

Before Tolkien could answer, the sound of Rex Dowling's harsh whisper pierced the night: "Here they come. Both parties." Torn back to the present, Tolkien and Fleming turned quickly and saw Hans and Jonas Kaufman coming toward them out of the forest at a low run. A quick look behind revealed Korumak, Gylfi, and Dagna, each carrying large tin cans in each hand, approaching at a quick walk through the orchard.

* * *

The fellowship, in its full complement of eleven, now knelt or sat on the ground in a semi-circle at the foot of the orchard wall. The six four-liter tins of lamp oil procured by the dwarfs were lined up behind them.

"You first," Fleming said to Korumak.

"All the German soldiers are dead," said Korumak, "except one, the radio operator. We subdued him."

"The priests?"

"I told them to leave, but they refused. They have no means of transport, some are old, some sick. None have left the abbey in twenty years."

"Did you tell them the Reich will likely be very angry at them?"

"They don't care. They say they will pray."

"The rat poison?"

"The cook used it all."

"Took no chances. Good man."

"Of course," said Dowling, "if autopsies are done, all of the monks will hang, as well as Father Schneider."

"Fleming shook his head. "Bloody hell."

"Hans?" Fleming said.

"Seven men at the Roman wall."

"The patrol," said Fleming. "They must have left one man back to man the radio."

"How did they know about the Roman wall, that the cave entrance was there?" said Dowling.

"They must have gotten it out of the abbot," said Fleming.

"Somehow I doubt that," Dowling replied. "I . . ." he said, but went no further, shaking his head.

"Shall we return and kill them?" said Hans.

"We have no choice," Fleming replied. "That's where the cave entrance is."

"The scouting was a good idea, I apologize," said Vaclav. When they reached the orchard the Czech captain had been all for going straight to the Roman wall, but Fleming and Dowling, counseling caution, had rejected that idea and sent Hans and Jonas out to scout.

"Jonas and I can do it," Hans said. "Wait here. Come when I whistle."

"No."

"Yes."

Professor Tolkien watched as Fleming considered what to do, gazing from him to Dowling, to the new man, Vaclav, who was grinning from ear to ear. He has no fear, Tolkien thought, he is literally fearless. What better trait to have in a soldier?

"I'll go with you," Vaclav said. "I will not take no for an answer. These may be the only Nazis we'll get a chance to kill tonight."

"The five of us will go," said Fleming, indicating himself, Dowling, Vaclav and the Kaufman brothers. "Come when I whistle twice," he said to Professor Shroeder and the others. "How far is it, Hans?"

"A hundred meters, no more."

"Can we surprise them?" Fleming asked. "Tell me the terrain."

"There is a small rise on the north side. The wall butts against a hill. They have cleared an area near the wall and spread out behind it at four foot intervals."

"Like they're guarding a fort," said Dowling.

"Yes," Hans replied. "If we can get to the ridge on the north without them detecting us, we can dispose of them with one hand grenade."

"Two," said Vaclav. "I will be throwing one as well."

Overhead they heard the sound of a plane approaching, a low flying plane from the sound of it. There had been complete silence, and then suddenly the harsh buzz of the plane's propeller. They scrambled to the wall and pressed themselves, faces down on the cold earth, against its large smooth stones. The plane flew over at no more than three hundred feet. A searchlight beam from its belly swept the wall and the nearby tree line. The plane flew off but only to bank and return, this time flying even lower, perhaps fifty feet above the treetops that surrounded the little orchard on three sides. The searchlight swept directly over them, then the plane climbed and flew away into the night.

"I don't get it," Rex Dowling said. "First they go north, then they come back here."

"They still have the radio at the abbey," Fleming replied. "I guess some survived the rat poison and called for instructions."

"Why send a recon plane? Why not just send troops?"

"I agree," said Fleming. "It doesn't matter though. They saw us, which means they'll be back in force."

"We're wasting time," said Vaclav. "We could be in the tunnel by now."

The five-man commando team crouched and waited for Fleming's signal. He raised his right hand and then lowered it sharply and they were off at a crouching run into the forest.

49.
Berlin
October 10, 1938, 12:15 a.m.

"*Ja*," said Reinhard Heydrich. "Yes, yes, *danke*. I will call you back in ten minutes."

Across from Heydrich on a plush couch sat Heinrich Himmler. He had just taken a sip of hock and was dabbing at his Hitleresque mustache with a linen napkin. They were at the end of Heydrich's large, rectangular office reserved for comfortable meetings with Nazis in the highest echelon. The rich, soft textured, one-hundred-thousand-dollar Persian rug that covered this area was sixty feet in length by forty feet in width. They were there to discuss an operation they were planning that would launch, once and for all, the mass incarceration and eventual elimination of all Jews in Germany. It was a celebration of sorts. They had worked hard to develop a group of "paramilitaries," basically civilian thugs with clubs, who would spearhead the operation in the major cities. The Munich Agreement had not even mentioned Jews or minorities, let alone provided any protection for them, but still, how could the German authorities expect to control a spontaneous uprising of the people of the kind they had so fastidiously planned? All they needed was an excuse, preferably the assassination of a popular German politician or soldier, the sort of thing that worked beautifully in the past to stir up popular hatred. If one didn't happen soon, they had agreed they would have the SS do it and then blame it on a radical, German-hating Jew.

"Who was that?" Himmler asked, hoping it wasn't something that would spoil their celebration.

"My adjutant. They have spotted our professors and at least nine others on the ground in Metten."

"I see. This is not good."

"No, the nearest troops are two hundred kilometers away."

"You will have to call Goering."

"Goering?"

"Yes, he can get paratroopers there in thirty minutes. Tell him it is a direct order from me."

"You are not his superior."

"If he refuses, tell him I will go directly to the Fuhrer. Everyone knows the Fuhrer will name me his successor. It's all but signed and sealed."

"How many troops?"

"Several hundred, blanket the area."

"Dead, or alive?"

"We want Shroeder alive, the others must all be killed."

"We don't know who they are."

"Reinhard, are you concerned? Is your mole among them?"

"Of course not."

"Good."

"Goering will want to share the glory."

"If his men catch Shroeder and we wrench his secret from him, our fat flyboy will deserve a share of the credit."

50.
The Bavarian Forest
October 9, 1938, 12:30 a.m.

Fleming and Professor Shroeder climbed over what was left of the Roman wall and walked slowly along the steep, rocky hillside that ran behind it for about a hundred yards. The others were back at the scene of the attack on the troops at the wall, a one-sided affair in which five hand grenades thrown simultaneously had made a bloody mess of the seven German soldiers whose fate it was to guard this long forgotten, two-thousand-year-old wall with their lives. Which is what they did, though they never knew why it was so important. The English reporter-cum-spy and the German professor were glad to leave that scene behind—body parts were everywhere, rock dust settling on them like shrouds.

"This is it," said Shroeder, stopping suddenly.

"Where?" said Fleming.

"That ledge. The entrance is behind it."

Fleming looked up at a small rock outcrop about thirty feet up the bramble-covered hill.

"Are you sure?" he said.

"Look at me," Shroeder said.

Fleming looked and saw the hair on the old man's head, white as snow and long, standing straight up, the professor's eyes an unnatural dark, dark green. "I'll get the others," he said.

"No, wait," said the professor.

Fleming, who had started to turn away, turned back.

"We must hurry. What is it?"

"I need your word that you will take care of Billie."

"You have it."

"That you will take her out of Germany."

"She may not agree to go."

"She has to, she is a Jew."

Fleming paused before answering, *yes, he had heard right.* "A Jew?" he said. "Nonsense, her mother was a Prussian aristocrat. She told me the story."

"That was a fairy tale I told her. Her mother was a Jewess in Munich, where I was teaching, a servant. I fell in love with her. We were to be married."

"Professor Shroeder . . ."

"She doesn't know, you see. Jews have never been loved in Germany. I thought it best . . . And then the Nazis came along."

"You have my word."

"Thank you. Fleming?"

"Yes."

"It was not my life I was in fear of losing. Would that I had lost it years ago. Bauer knows Billie is a Jew. He found the birth papers in Munich. He told me if I did not find the artifacts and perform the ritual, Billie would be sent to a concentration camp, where she would surely die. Tell me again, do I have your word?"

"Yes, professor, you do."

* * *

When Fleming returned with the others, Shroeder was crouching on the ledge, looking into the mouth of the tunnel. His hair had returned to its normal disheveled state and was now whipping in the wind that had suddenly started to gust. He turned to face them and, Moses-like, pointed down to them with his cane. If the journey from Berlin to Carinhall to Metten had taken its toll, he did not show it, at least not in his voice. "Come," he said, loudly and clearly, "John Ronald and Trygg and Gylfi and Dagna, no others. It is a long tunnel."

<u>51.</u>
The Devil's Canyon, October 9, 1938, 1:45 a.m.

John Ronald Tolkien stood next to Franz Horst Shroeder on a small, rocky shelf gazing down, and up, at the Devil's Canyon. The English professor's fevered imaginings of this place, based less on Franz Shroeder's brief description than on the exotic venues of his beloved Norse mythology, were nothing compared to the real thing. The width and breadth of a rugby pitch, its walls on all sides were sheer vertical stone covered almost to the top with a leafless, thorny vine. The same plant, if it could be called a plant, covered most of the canyon floor, except now it took the form of rambling brush and bramble, in places the height of a full-grown man. Only a raggedly circular area of a diameter of perhaps twenty-five feet, just below where he stood, remained bare earth. At the far end he could make out through the near complete darkness the shape of a gigantic tree, its top branches extending up and over the canyon's rim. The thorn-brambles surrounded the tree and were growing, in tortured, twisting patterns, up and around its massive trunk.

"The Devil's oak," said Shroeder.

"I don't see the alter."

"The torch."

Tolkien switched on the flashlight he had used to help negotiate the tunnel, where its white light was a godsend. Here its beam shone weakly to a point a few feet ahead but no more. "Worthless," he said.

"Give it to me," said Shroeder. "When the dwarfs are done, I will use it to find the alter."

Down on the canyon floor they could dimly make out Trygg, Gylfi, and Dagna hacking out three separate paths to the Devil's oak through the bramble with their maces, dragging their tins of lamp oil behind them as they went. Above they could hear the wind beginning to blow hard, much harder and steadier now than the gusts that buffeted them on the hillside before they entered the tunnel. The sky was covered with thick, heavy clouds.

"Why am I here, Franz?" Tolkien said. "Surely not to carry the torch."

"You are here to bear witness."

"Bear witness?"

"The world will need to know."

"What about Trygg, the dwarfs?"

"They will return to their mountain homes. They will never be heard from again."

"Never? I don't understand."

"It will be a thousand years before they mingle again with men."

Tolkien remained silent. He took a moment to gaze at the old man's face, in grim profile. *The face of a prophet,* he thought, *or a madman, or both.*

"I will start down," said Shroeder.

"I will come with you."

"No, John, this task is mine alone. You must stay here. When the dwarfs are done, I will send them here as well."

"I cannot let you . . ."

"*You can and you must,*" Shroeder boomed. He turned to face Tolkien head-on as he said this. "This is between me and Satan. Alone. Your presence will weaken me and strengthen him."

The Englishman looked into his friend's eyes, which were closed to mere slits. Tolkien caught a glimpse of the old man's once light brown but now piercing, black orbs floating behind these narrow openings. For several painful seconds, they bore through and beyond the Englishman, forcing him to look away. *He's not looking at me,* Tolkien thought, *he's looking into hell, anticipating this thing he must do.* The world of John Ronald Tolkien, the world of men, no longer existed for Franz Shroeder. *You may not see me, Franz,* Tolkien said to himself, *but I will stay here. I will not let you die.*

Tolkien watched as Shroeder turned away, descended the hill, and walked slowly into and across the small clearing to the edge of the bramble. The dwarfs were now making their way back along the rough paths they had cut, splashing lamp oil to either side as they did. Where this rough growth ended they met Professor Shroeder, who was stabbing his flashlight into the thorny branches all around him. The dwarfs spoke to him for a second and then they began to hack at the bramble with their razor sharp maces. In a few minutes they uncovered a dark, anvil-shaped stone as high as Shroeder's waste. The professor approached the stone and gestured to the dwarfs, who immediately withdrew the rust-colored pieces of flint and C-shaped pieces of steel they had brought with them. Scraping the flint against the steel, they began sending sparks into the oil-covered bramble. The bramble began almost immediately to smolder, but not burn. Again the professor and the dwarfs spoke and then the dwarfs headed back to join Tolkien on his shelf overlooking the canyon. Above, the wind was not just blowing hard, it was howling, emitting a high, thin, screeching sound, like the sound of souls dying or caught in the throes of agony.

The sound was so bad that Tolkien had to put his hands flat to his ears to try to block it out. He was standing like this when Trygg, Gylfi, and Dagna reached him. He nodded to them and then they all fixed their gazes on the scene below: the brambles smoldering with a dense gray smoke like the floor of hell, the wind screeching and howling, the clouds, dense and black, pressing down on the canyon like a massive lid barring all escape, and Franz Shroeder, standing to his full height, his hair blowing wildly in the wind, holding the amulet before him in one hand and the parchment in the other. Tolkien was astonished to hear snatches of his friend's booming voice above the unearthly din. *Vedo Retro Satana, Vedo Retro Satana, Vedo Retro Satana* . . .

"The brambles are not burning," said Korumak.

"I will go down," said Tolkien.

"No, you will surely die. Look!"

The dwarf pointed to the Devil's oak, where, high up, the wind had blown its branches into the shape of a face, the face of Satan. Rain was now falling, one or two large drops at first and then a few more. They could not take their eyes off the face in the giant oak, which now seemed to be grinning, laughing even.

Then from a huge black cloud above the tree came a single lightning bolt. Long and bright and sharp as a diamond, it struck the top of the tree and instantly ignited the smoldering brambles. Tolkien and the dwarfs were thrown back against the stone wall behind them by the heat and force of the lightning. When they staggered forward again and looked they saw Professor Shroeder lying on the ground next to the black stone alter. They watched, mesmerized, the rain falling heavier and heavier, as he dragged himself to his feet, walked a few steps toward the tree, and flung first the amulet and then the parchment into the flames that were licking at the base of its trunk. When the artifacts disappeared the entire tree burst into flames, sucking in an instant all of the oxygen, all of the life, out of the canyon. Suddenly unable to breathe, Tolkien and the dwarfs collapsed to the ground and crawled to the tunnel opening, which was only a few steps away.

When Tolkien was able to breathe again, sucking large drafts of air inside the cave, he gathered himself and crawled back to the shelf. He did not know how or when he decided to do this, but his right hand was inside his tunic. Fingering his Benedict medal, he looked upon the scene below. The entire canyon, end to end, was covered in a foot of thick, black, smoldering ash. The tree was gone, the alter stone was gone, the thorn brambles gone, and Franz Shroeder gone.

"I don't see him," he said to the dwarfs, who had followed him out. "We have to go down."

"No," Trygg Korumak said. "He's gone. His death was part of the ritual."

"No, it can't be."

"Yes," the dwarf replied. "It can be and it is. The Devil took one last human life from this place, but he will take no more. It has been cleansed by fire and blood."

52.

The Bavarian Forest
October 9, 1938, 1:45 a.m.

"They have been gone too long," said Dowling. "We should go in after them."

"No," said Fleming. "We'll wait."

The remaining members of the fellowship were posted in positions around the tunnel entrance; Fleming, Dowling, and Billie behind the Roman wall, Vaclav, Hans, and Jonas on the ledge above. Except for Billie, who was given a pistol, they all had machine guns slung around their shoulders, along with hand grenades on shoulder or web clips, and ammo belts crisscrossed over their chests. If the Germans attacked, they might eventually get into the tunnel, but they would pay a heavy price.

"Listen," said Dowling. "The planes are coming back." Ten minutes earlier they had heard the roar of large aircraft. They had looked up and within a few seconds could see the silhouettes of eleven planes approaching from the west under a thickening cloud cover perhaps a thousand feet above their heads. Fleming, using what he called his "blacklight" glasses, had identified them as Junkers JU 390 cargo planes.

Now Fleming put these experimental binoculars to his eyes again and after a moment said, "Yes, it's the same group."

"Cargo planes," said Dowling, "why cargo planes?"

"Because they carry paratroopers," Fleming replied. "Here they come."

"Christ," said Dowling. "How many?"

"I'd say two hundred," the Englishman replied, "twenty or so per plane. Look, you don't need glasses."

Dowling came over from his post to join Fleming and they both gazed through a gap in the treetops at the night sky filled with the silhouettes of soldiers drifting to earth under canopies of silk. Many were being blown far off course by gusts of wind. Some of these crashed into others, entangling their chutes and lines.

"They're crazy," said Dowling. "In *this* weather, *this* terrain. One in ten will make it to the ground alive."

"I agree," Fleming said. "Himmler must want these magic objects awfully badly. There are nothing but tall trees shoulder to shoulder for miles around."

Before Dowling could respond, the rain, at first in isolated, heavy drops and then almost immediately in torrents, began to fall, and the wind that had been blowing in sporadic gusts for the past fifteen or twenty minutes began to suddenly blow with almost tornadic violence. *That should take care of those parachute chaps,* Fleming said to himself, smiling. Then, before he could form another thought, he heard a sharp cracking sound on the hillside where Vaclav and the Kaufman brothers were stationed. He looked in the direction of this sound, and saw that a group of boulders above the tunnel entrance had been struck and unmoored from the earth by a felled tree, and that these boulders were now rolling downhill directly at him and his colleagues.

The five men and Billie froze for an instant at this sight, then scrambled madly to the left and right, as the rocks, perhaps twenty or thirty of all sizes, began caroming off the ledge in front of the tunnel entrance, breaking off chunks of earth and rock as they hit. Their next stop was the Roman wall thirty feet below.

Fleming caught up with Billie as he dashed away from the cascading boulders and dragged her with him to safety, covering her with his body as they hit the ground. When the last rock landed, he waited a second or two and looked up. The avalanche had smashed a large swath of the Roman wall to unrecognizable bits, which were strewn everywhere. The boulders themselves lay in a large pile where the wall had been. Visibility beyond the immediate area was almost zero in the rain and the dark. He stood and slipped in the mud underfoot to his knees, stood and slipped again, and then crawled through mud and water up toward the ledge. At the top he was jolted to see a body slumped over its stony outcrop. *Hans*. A few feet away, Vaclav was kneeling over a prone body. "Jonas. Dear God," Fleming said out loud, the closest he had come to a prayer since he was a boy.

"Ian," Billie called out, "what is it?"

"Hans and Jonas," he shouted back. "They're hurt. Stay there."

Fleming climbed onto the ledge on his belly, then crawled through the howling wind and pelting rain to help Hans. With strength he did know he had, he dragged the war veteran back onto the ledge and turned him on his back. The top of Hans' head was a bloody mess. When Fleming attempted to clean the blood away with his hand, he felt something hard and gritty. *Bone*. He pulled his hand away and saw Hans' brain exposed through a large crack in his skull. *Dead*, he said to himself.

"Jonas is dead too," a voice behind him said.

Turning, Fleming saw Dowling crouching behind him, muddy rainwater mixed with blood streaming down his face.

"Are you okay?" Fleming asked.

"Yes. Billie?"

"Okay."

They both turned to look over at Vaclav, who was standing on the ledge with his hands pressed against a large boulder. He was also covered in mud and blood.

"The tunnel," Vaclav shouted. "The tunnel. It's gone."

Before they could respond, the hillside was lit to incandescence by the light from a lightning bolt striking somewhere nearby, a strike that caused the very earth under them to tremble, the jolting force of which tossed Fleming, Dowling, and Vaclav off the ledge like they were rag dolls.

53.

The Bavarian Forest
October 9, 1938, 2:00 a.m.

"We could throw hand grenades at it," said Dowling.

"That would probably make things worse," Fleming replied. "Not to mention drawing any paratroopers who survived to us."

"It's a matter of simple physics," said Vaclav.

They turned in unison to look at the Czech.

"We wedge it out of the way," he said.

"With what?"

"The felled tree," Vaclav replied, pointing.

At their feet, among the rubble that was once a section of the Roman wall, lay what was left of the tree that had started the boulder avalanche. Its branches and most of its bark ground off as it had rolled along amidst the wildly tumbling stones, one end sheared raggedly where it had broken in half, the other end a ball of muddy stump. It was perhaps twenty feet long and two feet in diameter. They then turned their collective gaze to the boulder that was blocking the tunnel entrance.

"It could be done," said Dowling.

"Let's give it a lift," Fleming said.

They spread out along the tree and, at the Englishman's count of three, lifted it with relative ease to waist high.

"Down," Fleming said.

They put it down and again looked up at the boulder.

"The ground is all mud up there," said Vaclav. "We could undermine it on one end, while wedging the tree in at the other."

54.

The Bavarian Forest
October 9, 1938, 2:15 a.m.

"We could go back," said Professor Tolkien. "Climb out. Franz found a way."

"That was sixty years ago," said Korumak. "Besides, none of us could make it an inch up those sheer walls."

"Do you hear something?" Dagna asked.

"What?" the others said. "No."

"Listen."

They had made it, after a long, slow uphill trek, back to the tunnel entrance, only to find it completely blocked by what looked like one large boulder, and had been discussing their limited options ever since. Now they stood mutely and listened for whatever Dagna had heard, but nothing but stony silence reached their ears.

"Nothing," said Korumak, who had made a small pitch torch—from what materials Tolkien did not know—which he now raised nearer to the boulder and then above it and down both sides.

"Not a crack," he said. "Not a breath of air."

"Do you know of any other caves or tunnels that would get us out?" Tolkien asked. "You've been in this part of the world before, that much is obvious."

"There were many caves and tunnels in this forest when I first explored it," the dwarf said. "But that was long ago, and I remember nothing but this one that leads in and out of the Devil's Canyon."

"How long ago was that?" Tolkien asked.

"Before you were born, Professor."

"How long before?"

"If we ever meet again," Korumak said, "I will tell you my age, but not now, not tonight. The mountain gods would not approve."

"The mountain gods. I see."

"You don't of course."

"I don't."

"You are writing a book, Professor, are you not?" Korumak asked. "A trilogy."

"A trilogy?" Tolkien answered. "No such thing. A novel."

"There is magic in threes," Korumak said, his eyes twinkling. "Like the three dwarfs who helped defeat Lucifer tonight in his own backyard. Perhaps I am three hundred years old . . ."

"Hush!" said Dagna. "I *do* hear something."

55.

The Bavarian Forest
October 9, 1938, 2:30 a.m.

"I think it moved," said Dowling.

"It did," said Billie.

Three of them—Dowling, Fleming, and Billie—were standing on the ledge on alternate sides
along the length of the tree, which was wedged at its
broken end under the boulder. Vaclav, who seemed
inexhaustible to the others, was standing at the far
end holding the muddy stump on his shoulder. They
had first used rocks and branches to scrape away a
great deal of muddy earth from beneath one end of
the large rock and then the other. At the second dig,
they stuck the tree end in and began to push and lever, push and lever, slipping often in the mud at their
feet. All of the force they applied was human, coming
from the muscles of their arms and chests. All were
bruised and bloody from their frantic scraping at the
ground and from using their arms to scrape away
rubble. All were covered with mud.

They stopped now to breathe and to take in what
Billie and Dowling had just said. Could it be?

"One more heave," said Vaclav.

They obeyed and gasped when the boulder
inched forward.

"One more!" said Vaclav.

This time the boulder, which they had estimated weighed a thousand pounds, inched again, paused for a long second, and then rolled, very slowly at first, but eventually with great speed, down the hillside where it came to an unclimactic stop among the boulders and rubble where the wall had been.

Watching the boulder, they had all forgotten to look inside the tunnel, but there was no need. Out stepped Tolkien and the three dwarfs. All were smiling, happy to be saved, until they saw Billie's face.

"He had to die, Miss Lillian," said Korumak. "There was no other way."

<u>56.</u>
Metten Abbey
October 9, 1938, 3:00 a.m.

The gates of Metten Abbey were wide open. In the courtyard a hulking Daimler sedan sat like a prehistoric creature under the portico that protected the front door from the elements. It had stopped raining, but a German soldier in a poncho was standing under this cover, leaning against the car, smoking. His back was to them.

"That's a staff car," said Fleming.

"It's Kurt Bauer's," said Billie. "I recognize it."

"What's a lieutenant doing with a staff car?" said Dowling. "Or a *staff*, for that matter."

They were crouched behind the abbey wall at the gate. The courtyard remained strewn with rubble, wet now and muddy from all the rain, but the bodies— Father Wilfrid, the German gunner, the German sergeant—were all gone. The wind had died to nothing. Moonlight shone through clouds that were rapidly breaking up overhead.

"Someone sent him on a wild goose chase, and now he's back," said Fleming. "His troops can't be far behind."

"No time to waste," said Dowling.

"I agree," said Fleming. "Vaclav, is there a road near the landing field?"

"Yes, east-west. The pilot used it as a landmark."

"How far?"

"A half-kilometer."

"How long will he wait?"

"Say 5:00 a.m. He needs to fly back in the dark."

"Trygg, can you help us one last time?"

"Of course."

"Go around to the left. Make some noise. Draw the guard to you. Vaclav, you and I will get into that stand of trees there. We kill the guard when he gets near. No guns, no noise."

A few moments later, the sound of stones hitting the left side of the abbey could be distinctly heard. The German soldier looked that way and was about to take a drag from his cigarette when the sound came again. This time he flipped the cigarette away, shouldered his rifle, and headed over to take a look. He stopped at the corner of the abbey and unslung his weapon. Now more stones came flying right at him and he flattened against the building's massive stone wall. He was edging back to the portico when the handle of an ax suddenly appeared in his chest. He slumped where he was.

At the front door a German officer appeared.

"Kurt," said Billie, who was crouching at the gate with Dowling. They watched as Bauer looked left and right, then peered into the car. He stepped back and walked slowly around the car. When he made his full circuit, he started walking slowly to the left. Fleming, Dagna, Trygg and Gylfi were now approaching the gate at a crawl, hugging the wall.

"They didn't see Bauer," Dowling said.

Before Billie could answer, the American stood and began running straight at the German lieutenant. Hearing the sound of this running, Bauer turned and, seeing Dowling racing toward him, tried to get his pistol out of its leather holder. Before he could unsnap the ebony clasp that held it closed, Dowling leaped on him and they tumbled to the ground amidst the rubble. They got to their feet and again the German went for his gun, this time getting it out.

Dowling ducked and lunged at him and they both hit the turret wall. Bauer's gun went clattering onto the cobblestones.

At the gate, Fleming unslung his machine gun, but could not take a chance on hitting Dowling. All three dwarfs had their hands on their axes, but were likewise stymied. They watched as Dowling took a blow from Bauer's fist and staggered back, hitting the ground hard and rolling onto his stomach. As Dowling got to his knees the German lowered his head and rushed him. As the blow struck, Dowling grabbed Bauer's head and wrenched it violently to the left. Bauer landed on top of the American, but the fight was out of him. Dowling shoved him off, got to his knees and looked down at the German whose head was sideways, his neck obviously broken. He was still breathing.

Fleming and Vaclav now appeared at Dowling's side. They could hear Bauer's ragged breathing. "Finish him," said Fleming, but Vaclav was ahead of him. He had already drawn his knife. "Gladly," he said, as he bent and slit Kurt Bauer's throat with one silky stroke.

"Gentleman!"

They turned toward the front door, toward the sound of this voice, where they saw a monk walking toward them.

"Are there other German soldiers in the abbey?" Fleming asked when the monk, a short, stout man in his forties, reached them.

"No," the monk replied, "but they are on their way. The whole battalion will be here any moment. The lieutenant came ahead to prepare."

"What did you do with all the bodies?"

"We dragged them into the woods. Father Wilfrid we buried."

"Do you know this area, Father?" Fleming asked.

"Yes," the priest replied. "I was born and raised in Deggendorf."

"There is a farm about four kilometers east. Do you know it? How do we get there? What road?"

"Yes, the Kruger farm. It's the same road you came in on," the monk answered. "Go east—left—when you exit the abbey. It goes directly to Czechoslovakia."

"How will we know the farm?"

"The farm is deserted. No lights. But you will see a silo—a round barn—in the distance on your right. They grew wheat there once. Excuse me now," the monk said, kneeling over Bauer. "I must pray for this man's soul."

"You're wasting your time," Fleming said, "he doesn't have one."

Then, turning to Dowling, he said, "it would be nice if the keys were in the car."

57.

The Kruger Farm, Outside Deggendorf
October 9, 1938, 3:30 a.m.

"That's a roadblock up ahead," said Vaclav.

"And there's the silo," said Billie.

Fleming slowed to a stop. "Have they spotted us?" he said.

"Maybe not," said Dowling. "Without headlights."

They had slowly made their way in the dark to what they guessed would be the vicinity of the farm, the thick forest on either side of the road having given way to open fields. The half moon that had been dodging storms and storm clouds all night now shone brightly through a clear, still night.

"I'll look," said Fleming.

The others, Vaclav in the front, Billie, Dowling, and Tolkien in the back, and the dwarfs in the third row of seats, facing the rear, watched as Fleming got out his blacklight glasses, exited the car, and climbed onto its roof. He was back in under a minute.

"Well," said Vaclav.

"I think they spotted us. They're scurrying around."

"Where did you get those glasses?" Vaclav asked. "Marvelous."

"A friend at MI-6. He's inventing things all the time."

"They're marvelous," said Dowling, "but what do we *do*?"

"Let us off here," said Korumak.

"Let you off?" said Fleming.

"Yes. And turn your headlights on."

"I assume you'll be leaving us," said Professor Tolkien.

"Yes, we will be," Korumak replied. "But we will do you one last turn."

"Which would be?" said Fleming.

"The Germans will see you stopped with your lights on," the dwarf replied. "They will approach. When they get close, head quickly across this field into the farm. We will delay the Germans."

"And then be on your way?" Dowling said.

"One ride in a plane is enough for one lifetime I assume," said Tolkien. "However long that lifetime may be."

"Correct, Professor," said Korumak. "We flew once to help Professor Shroeder, but now he is dead and our mission is done. No more flying for dwarfs."

"Thank you," said Fleming. "Farewell."

"I've given Professor Tolkien a farewell gift," said Korumak. "It may come in handy."

"How will you get away?" Billie asked.

"Easily," Korumak replied. "No man alive can track us."

"Goodbye then," said Korumak. He had been standing, facing the front. Now Gylfi and Dagna stood as well. All three were holding small axes— their backpacks were full of them—in each hand. Dagna and Gylfi nodded goodbye as well, and the dwarfs leaped from the car and dove quickly into the high brush that had run alongside the road for miles.

Fleming turned the Daimler's headlamps on and put his night vision glasses to his eyes. "They're coming," he said, a moment later.

"*What's* coming?" Vaclav asked.

"An open troop carrier."

"What do they hold?"

"How many, you mean?"

"Yes, how many troops?"

"Twenty probably."

When the troop truck was about fifty feet away, it stopped and ten or twelve soldiers jumped out of the back and fanned out on either side, their machine guns aimed at the Daimler. When they started to approach, the Englishman hit the accelerator hard and turned to the right. The Germans immediately began firing, but, looking in his rearview mirror, Fleming saw that six of them were felled with axes in the blink of an eye, and that the truck, when it tried to turn to give chase, could not move. *Axes to the tires*, Fleming thought, grinning. Then he hit the accelerator even harder.

Within seconds they were flying past the abandoned farmhouse and silo, heading toward a thick line of trees, on the other side of which Fleming hoped was the landing field and the plane to extract them.

"Can we drive through those trees?" Vaclav asked.

"No, too thick," Fleming answered.

In another moment they were stopped and leaping out of the car. In another they were at the edge of the landing field, which was bathed in silvery moonlight, but which did not contain an airplane.

"No plane," said Dowling.

"What's that, there on the right, under the trees?" said Vaclav. "Is that it?"

"It could be," said Dowling.

"Let's go see," said Fleming.

Suddenly, behind them, they heard the sound of multiple truck engines approaching; then, in quick succession, the slamming of doors and the sound of many harsh voices barking out in German.

"They radioed back," said Fleming.

The fellowship turned and crouched in unison, and now could plainly see perhaps sixty or seventy soldiers spread out and walking slowly into the tree line, about fifty yards away.

"Spread out," said Fleming. "Fire on my command."

Only Fleming, Vaclav, and Dowling had machine guns. Billie had her Luger. Professor Tolkien had no weapon, but as the Germans approached he pulled the small glass vial that Korumak had given him in the car out of his tunic pocket. *Break it on a rock and throw it*, the dwarf had said.

"Fire!" Fleming said.

The Germans hit the ground at this initial burst, some of them dead or wounded, but most of them just taking cover. One or two fired in the fellowship's direction from their prone positions.

"They can't see us, we can't see them," said Vaclav.

"What's that?" said Billie.

A rocket had risen from the German line. *A mortar this close,* thought Fleming, but when it burst above their heads he realized it was a flare, its bright light exposing them for several excruciatingly long seconds.

"Look!" said, Billie. "The plane."

They turned quickly and saw the Avia lumbering out of the woods on the left, heading toward them.

"They're coming!" said Dowling.

All turned again to see a swarm of German infantrymen charging directly at them through the trees, crouching low, firing their weapons.

Professor Tolkien, remembering the night he failed to go back for Major Val Fleming, remained calm. He broke the vial on a nearby rock and flung it at the oncoming German soldiers. At first it trailed a streak of blue flame behind it, then it suddenly burst into an immense cloud of smoke, a thick gray cloud that covered an area fifty yards in all directions, from the ground to the treetops.

Seeing this huge cloud blinding and disorienting the Germans, hearing them calling out helplessly in its midst, the fellowship, now down to five, rose as one and raced headlong for the plane, which had reached their end of the field and was turning to line

226

up for takeoff. Tolkien was the last one to reach the door in the belly behind the cockpit. Fleming and Dowling grabbed his hands and hoisted him up.

With just a few feet to spare at the end of the field, the plane lifted off, skimmed over the forest, and began to climb.

EPILOGUE
Prague
December 20, 1938, 7:00 p.m.

Ian Fleming stood—scotch in one hand, Morland's Special in its holder in the other—at the room's floor-to-ceiling French doors, looking down at Prague in its Christmas glory. The Mala Strana, just below, the Charles Bridge in the mid-ground, and the Old Town Square in the distance, all sparkled like clusters of many-colored jewels on a velvet carpet. In Wenceslas Square, to the right, the gold sheathing covering the equestrian statue in its center seemed on fire as it reflected the white lights that were strung in thickly woven strands all around it. Fleming had walked to Old Town Square in the morning, to a tobacconist's to pick up his weekly shipment of cigarettes from Morland. The small shop was on a narrow street off the square, more of an alley than a proper street, but nevertheless still garlanded from storefront to storefront on both sides with holiday green and red and gold. He had paused when he saw the grim set of the shop owner's face, and thought, yes, your last Christmas before you are enslaved. The real madness is about to start.

In Fleming's jacket pocket was a letter from Professor Tolkien, brought round that morning by the British Embassy courier. Patting his breast, he thought now of Tolkien's penultimate paragraph. *I did not think I'd make it home, but now that I have, I feel it is the sweetest place on earth, made infinitely sweeter because in England we breathe the air of freedom. I had forgotten the cost of this freedom until our glimpse into the dark heart of Nazi Germany. Though neither young nor spry nor trained in anything useful, I would consider it a great favor if you would contact me in future if you think my services could be of even the slightest assistance, at home or abroad.*

Ian Fleming had never taken to the stiff-necked type of freedom practiced by his father and grand-father, both more Scotsmen than Englishmen. Too much responsibility, too much self-denial. Too little fun. No fun, really. But now, recalling the old tobac-conist's face and reading Tolkien's unabashedly sen-timental words, responsibility and self-denial did not seem like such bad things, especially given the alter-native of servitude to Hitler and his madmen.

A movement to his left shook Fleming from his reverie. Turning, he was shocked to see Eldridge White standing at the room's one doorway looking in his direction. He took a step toward White, but stopped when he saw the tall, white-maned, former marine raise his right hand palm up. *Stay put.* There were only three other people in the hotel's small sitting room, a couple in a rear corner and a waiter in a white waist jacket handing them a bill to sign. When they did and were gone, the waiter as well, White pointed to a set of comfortable chairs near the fireplace.

Not to worry, old chap, Fleming said to himself, as he walked to the chairs. *You've met him before; he and your dad were chums.* Still, the chief of MI-6, his identity known to the king, the prime minister, and perhaps a dozen other people in the world, old Ellie White himself, here to see him? Not possible. Must be some other business. They reached the chairs at the same time, shook hands silently, and sat.

"I must say . . ." said Fleming

"You're surprised."

"Shocked. What brings you here?"

"You."

"Me. I daresay . . ."

"How are you?"

"Fine. Couldn't be better. Waiting for Billie. Hot soak, makeup, you know the drill. Having a smoke and a drink."

"Fraulein Shroeder."

"Yes, that's the one." Fleming attempted an off-hand smile, but he knew he didn't get it right. *What in God's name?*

"I have some news," said White, "that I felt obliged to deliver personally."

Mother, Fleming thought, *Peter, Michael, Richard.*

"Your family is well," said White. "It's not that."

"That's a relief."

"Sorry to frighten you."

Ian shook his head and smiled a real smile. "Mother's not quite done molding me yet, you see. They all have their whack at it."

"You had quite an adventure, I'm told, in Germany."

"Quite."

"That's why I'm here."

"I sent a full report."

"It's something the Americans have brought up. Something new."

"I can't guess."

"I suppose not. Indeed, I'm delighted you can't guess."

Fleming was still a bit confused, but now more confident. His mother and brothers were alive and well. Though he had made no mention of heroics of any kind in his report to Bletchley House, he had been given decent marks by his superiors there, who had said, in effect, that though the occult wasn't usually their game, all had turned out well. They had even talked, jokingly, of he and Tolkien working together in future. Or were they serious? Old John Ronald had done rather well, they had said, a mad scientist of sorts. Smart, too, well above old Fleming's rank.

"Well . . ." said Fleming.

"The Americans," said White. "They've been in touch concerning an extraction operation they were supporting in Bremen. Ring a bell?"

"No, sorry."

"There was supposed to be a Krupp engineer in Magdaberg. Working on a tank coating."

"Oh, yes," said Fleming, his brow knitted.

"They passed a number to you, and a contact code."

"Yes."

"While you were in the woods in Bavaria, the operation was raided by the Gestapo. Four killed, four took cyanide."

Fleming had not really been looking at White, the hero of the Great War, the man who in 1928 had infiltrated Mussolini's inner circle, seduced his mistress, and assassinated the head of his secret police, the infamous OVRA. Not the front man, Francesco Nudi, but the real head, a deeply secret madman even the most hardened fascists were afraid of. It was too much like looking at the sun. You'd go blind. But now he looked, and did not like what he saw.

"Who did you give that number to?" Ellie White asked.

"I gave it to . . ."

"Yes, to whom?"

In Fleming's pocket was a diamond ring in a small satin and velvet box. He was going to ask Billie to marry him tonight, end his profligacy for good.

"To Billie Shroeder."

"Thank goodness," said White. "Washington thought it might be you."

"*Me.* You mean . . ."

"We told them to bugger off."

"Here," White said. He took a brown envelope from the inside pocket of his suit jacket and handed it to Fleming.

"What is it?"

"Telegraph receipts, two of them."

231

"Telegraph receipts?"

"We sent someone to Deggendorf. The telegraph office is in a chemist's shop. You know the Germans, how they multi-task. *'Poor us, you raped us at Versailles, we have to make a penny go a long way.'* They're also efficient to a fault, never throw away a receipt. Your Miss Shroeder sent two telegrams while you were in town, both to Heydrich."

"I . . ."

"Yes, I know, you're not sure what to do. Not to worry, we'll take care of it. Take your time."

Ian Fleming would never again be at a loss for words, but at this moment he was as silent as death, unable to formulate a coherent thought let alone a sentence.

"Did you ever tell her she was a Jew?" White asked.

Fleming remained silent.

"We'll take care of that as well."

* * *

Fleming stood for a long moment outside the door to his room, recalling, with an odd equanimity, as if they really had nothing to do with him, the reports and telegram copies that Ellie White had given him before taking his leave. Coming out of the lift he had passed two waiters he had never seen before, in waist jackets and bow ties, standing idly next to food service carts. Key in hand, he looked over and saw that they were still there. One nodded to him. Finally, he inserted the key and entered the room, his hand on the 20 caliber Beretta he carried with him at all times when not working, the safety off. Billie was on her back on the bed, dead, in her silk robe, one long, beautiful leg exposed, her eyes open. Papers and a brown envelope were scattered on the floor. He picked them up and glanced at them. A birth certificate, copies of the same telegrams he had just read and then burned in the lavatory downstairs, a list of eight people who worked at a textile company in Bremen.

He packed his things carefully, then looked at himself in the room's tall mirror. He had dressed, not formally, but what he considered *sparsely*, for the occasion of his engagement, his simple, no frills suit a deep charcoal, nearly black, his thin tie the same color, his shirt a snowy white, his cap-toed shoes black and highly polished. Appropriate, he thought, without irony. At the bed he reached over to close Billie's eyes, but paused first to look into them, now flat and lifeless as glass. "Old Ellie thought he was doing me a favor, Billie," he said, "but he wasn't. I wish he had left you to me." He decided to leave her eyes open. He had read somewhere that the soul had no peace until the dead body's eyes were closed.

In the hall outside the room were the two waiters he had never seen before. They nodded to him.

"A favor," said Fleming.

"If we can," said one.

"Leave her eyes open."

"That we can do."

Then Fleming stepped between them and headed to the lift.

About the Authors

James LePore is an attorney who has practiced law for more than two decades. He is also an accomplished photographer. He lives in Florida with his wife, artist Karen Chandler. He is the author of five other novels, *A World I Never Made*, *Blood of My Brother*, *Sons and Princes*, *Gods and Fathers*, and *The Fifth Man*, as well as a number of shorter works. You can visit him at his website, www.JamesLeporeFiction.com.

Carlos Davis wrote and produced films, among them the Emmy-nominated *Rascals and Robbers* with David Taylor and the cult favorite *Drop Dead Fred* with Tony Fingleton. He died in 2020.

The story continues in

GOD'S FORMULA

It is 1939. The scourge that is Nazi Germany is trampling Europe as its scientists vie to deliver ever-increasing destructive power. Now physicist Walter Friedeman – a friend of Albert Einstein's since childhood – has found a formula to enrich uranium in three months rather than the previously expected five years. Such a formula could deliver Germany the first atomic arsenal. But Friedeman does not believe in the Nazi cause. Friedeman wants the formula in the hands of America, but getting it to them himself will be nearly impossible. He sets into motion a plan to use his teenaged son, a Hitler Youth, to unwittingly do the job using a message Friedeman has encoded in the Elvish language created by J.R.R. Tolkien in his novel *The Hobbit*.

What follows is a quest across continents as Einstein, Tolkien, and MI-6 officer Ian Fleming work together to find Friedeman's son, decode the message, and wrest control of the nuclear future before Hitler can steal it for himself.

Reuniting Tolkien and Fleming after their adventure in *No Dawn for Men*, *God's Formula* is a heart-pounding thriller filled with history both real and imagined.

Read an excerpt on the following pages:

"So, William, what brings you here?"

"War is coming."

"Any day now."

"Roosevelt needs to know your state of readiness."

"It's nil."

"I know. I've told him. But that's not why I called you."

"I'm all ears."

Shaded by a large sycamore, Ian Fleming and Bill Donovan sat over tea on the rear terrace of Fleming's flat in Belgravia.

"Our people in Berlin have been contacted by a German scientist," the American said, "who wants to defect."

"Is he important?"

"Have you heard of the atomic bomb?"

"Vaguely."

"He's been working on it."

"You have people in Berlin, certainly."

"Yes, but that's just it. Roosevelt says no."

"You want us to do it?"

"Well…"

"Why not you?"

"Six months ago…"

"Yes."

"We thought Friedeman was a Jew."

"You were approached then?" Fleming asked.

"Yes, by Albert Einstein."

"And you turned him down?"

"Yes, my government did."

"You thought it was a Jew looking after a Jew."

"Something like that."

"But our man's not Jewish."

"No."

"The ironies abound."

"The UK has not exactly opened its doors."

"I agree. And why not now?"

"Hitler's cooking up a reason to invade Poland. We don't want to give him a reason to declare war on us as well."

"I see, but Poland is our ally, so if we get caught, what's the difference? We'll be at war with Germany soon anyway. Is that it?"

"Yes, I'm afraid that's Roosevelt's thinking."

"*Real politique.*"

"Yes. Hard as nails."

"Are we in urgent mode?"

"Yes, I'm afraid so. Our man believes he is being watched, that he will be arrested quite soon, that his formula will be discovered or tortured out of him."

"How did you come by all this?"

"In March I asked one of our people—your old friend Rex Dowling—to make contact. He did. Our scientist contacted Dowling last night. I should say early this morning. He's in panic mode."

"I'll run it by the old man."

Donovan remained silent. Sunlight, filtering through the old tree's thick branches, cast dappled shadows on the small table's snowy-white cloth covering.

They sipped their tea and the silence stretched out.

"I'll be discrete," the Englishman said, finally.

"Thank you."

"Did I hear it from you?"

"Yes, but I made no request."

"You mentioned it in passing."

"Something like that."

"What's the man's name?"

"Friedeman. Walter Friedeman."

The two men stared at each other over their tea-cups, their faces masks of politeness. Then Fleming put his cup down, extracted a Morland's Special from its packet, tamped it on the table, placed it snugly into its holder, and lit it.

"What's your interest?" he asked after taking a long drag and exhaling it with obvious pleasure.

"Personally?"

"Yes."

"Einstein."

"What about him?"

"He said Friedeman had found a way to make the bomb in three months."

"Three months. Bloody hell. And you believed him?"

"Yes. He's Einstein for God's sake."

"I thought he was a pacifist."

"That's just it. That's what sold me. He sees disaster coming and has been forced to change his principles. To bend them actually. He thinks the a-bomb would be better off in our hands than in Hitler's."

"If we get this bomb…"

"We're a long way from that."

"Yes, but if we do."

"You'll use it."

"We're a small island. Hitler's a mad man. I daresay we will."

"As I said, Albert is obviously willing to bend."

"It's an old story, Colonel. More tea? A bit of a bracer?" The Englishman had his hand on a bottle of St. George's.

Donovan looked at his watch.

"Do us good," said Fleming. "What with war coming and not being ready. Turn to the bottle."

Wild Bill Donovan smiled and slid his teacup toward his host. "Let me know what Godfrey says," he said. "I'll do what I can to help."

Get your copy of God's Formula wherever books are sold.